Mistaken
Love

Isaac Nkrumah Darko

Published by Revival Waves of Glory Books & Publishing

PO Box 596 | Litchfield, Illinois 62056 USA

www.revivalwavesofgloryministries.com

Revival Waves of Glory Books & Publishing is committed to excellence in the publishing industry.

Published in the United States of America

ISBN 978-1-68411-106-0

CHAPTER ONE

Pimso was an industrial city which was inhabited by people from all walks of life. People liked to live there because of the existence of many social and economic infrastructural facilities. At night, the illuminations of the streets made the city look very beautiful and worth living. One of the major economic infrastructural facilities which had made Pimso well known and attracted many people there was a gold mining company called Great Pillar. Great Pillar, as a big mining company, employed many people including the people of Pimso, thereby reducing unemployment rate and its attendant problems such as armed robbery, malnutrition and poverty in Pimso and its neighbouring towns and villages.

As people migrated to Pimso to look for jobs, a twenty-six-year-old man, Amoako who had graduated from university also made up his mind to go there to look for a job in the gold mining company. Thus, one day, early in the morning, he packed his possessions into a bag and set out on the journey to Pimso. As he walked majestically in his gorgeous dress to the car station to board a car, a twelve-year-old boy ran to collect his bag which he was holding in his right hand.

'Mr. Amoako, where are you going?' the boy asked.

'I'm going to the car station,' Amoako answered.

'May I take your bag there for you?' the boy asserted.

'Yes,' Amoako replied and handed the bag to the boy.

When they were about to reach the car station, a mate of a car rushed to collect the bag from the boy.

'Where are you going?' the mate asked.

'I'm going to Pimso,' Amoako answered.

'Then follow me. My car is going there,' the mate remarked and escorted Amoako to the car.

As the boy departed from Amoako to the house, Amoako called out to him.

'Boy! Boy! Come here.'

The boy then ran back to Amoako.

'Here I am,' he said.

'I've something for you,' Amoako said and unzipped his wallet, took Ten Ghana Cedis from it and gave it to him.

'It is okay. If I collect the money, it will mean that I'm charging you for bringing your luggage to the station,' the boy explained when he had refused to accept the money.

'Don't think that I'm paying you for bringing my luggage to the station. I'm giving you the money as an appreciation but not as a payment,' Amoako explained.

'If that is so, then I'll accept it,' the boy remarked.

Amoako having given the money to the boy remarked, 'You are well trained and cultured.'

'Thank you,' the boy asserted.

'What is the fare from here to Pimso?' Amoako asked the mate.

'It is Fifteen Ghana Cedis,' the mate answered.

Amoako unzipped his wallet again and took Fifteen Ghana Cedis from it to pay the fare.

When the car was full of passengers, the driver who was eager to reach Pimso within the shortest possible time drove the car at a high speed. After fifteen minutes of driving, the clouds gathered; it showed signs of rain. The wind which was turbulent caused trees to sway. The clouds became slightly dark and eventually it started raining amid lightning and thunder. When the driver was negotiating a curve, the car skidded off the road which nearly caused an accident. The situation made the passenger nervous, so they asked the driver to exercise caution and slow down.

'Driver, why are you driving recklessly like that? You must slow down,' a woman yelled.

'Ah! Driver, why are you speeding? Do you want us to lose our lives by your reckless driving? You must slow down,' a man shrieked and the driver slowed down until they reached Pimso. When Amoako alighted from the car, he picked up his mobile phone from his pocket and called his friend Sarpong to meet him.

'Hello, it is Amoako who is speaking. I've just arrived at Pimso and I'm at the station. May you come to take me home?' asked Amoako.

'Wait for me there. Don't go to any place. I'll be there very soon to take you home,' the friend asserted.

While Amoako was making the phone call, a young man, Akoto, secretly went to stand behind him and snatched his bag from him and ran away.

'Thief, catch him, catch him!' Amoako shouted while he ran after Akoto, but he couldn't catch him.

Akoto escaped and went to sit under a coconut tree and forcefully opened the bag. As he searched through the things in the bag, he found a bundle of banknotes and took it and counted it.

Being very happy, Akoto went to a restaurant to eat. As soon as he got seated, the waitress approached him and showed him the menu.

'Good morning, sir,' the waitress greeted.

'Good morning,' Akoto responded.

'May I know what you want?' the waitress inquired.

'I want the most sumptuous dish on the menu,' Akoto requested.

'Most of the dishes are sumptuous, so I can't determine which one will suit your budget and liking,' the waitress explained.

'Give me rice and stew and a bottle of Malta Guinness,' Akoto demanded.

Without delay, the waitress served Akoto with the food and the drink after he had paid for it.

In the night, Akoto disguised himself; he wore a mask on his face and special clothes and broke into a certain businesswoman's room and attacked her by inserting a gun into her left ear.

'Don't shout. Where do you keep your money?' Akoto demanded.

The woman, who was afraid, trembled uncontrollably and took a bag which contained money and handed it to Akoto.

'This is the bag which contains my money,' the woman muttered.

'Open it for me to see it?' Akoto instructed.

The woman, who was still trembling, opened the bag.

'See it,' she ordered.

'How much is the money?' Akoto thundered.

'It is Thirty Thousand Ghana Cedis,' the woman retorted.

'Close the bag and give it to me,' Akoto ordered.

Akoto, upon collecting the money from the woman, absconded away.

CHAPTER TWO

Five days later, Akoto who was walking on the street of Ankaasi, his hometown met a young woman whom he had a conversation with. The woman was an evangelist who was going home after evangelism. She was holding a Bible.

'Praise the Lord!' Akoto greeted.

'Amen!' the woman responded.

'Holding a Bible at this time of the day suggests that you are a woman of God,' Akoto said.

'Yes,' the woman answered.

'Then may I ask you a question which baffles me?' Akoto requested.

'Not really. I'm in a hurry,' the woman asserted.

'In a hurry?' Akoto exclaimed.

'Yes, but your question is about what?' the woman inquired.

'It is about the word of God,' replied Akoto.

'Then you can ask the question,' the woman asserted.

'What is the ultimate duty of man on this earth?' asked Akoto.

'It is recorded in Ecclesiastes 12:13 that ...*fear God and keep his commandments, for this is the whole duty of man...*'the woman answered.

'You have answered it correctly. You have spiritual understanding of the Scripture. I can see that you have much zeal for the work of God. Our elders say you can tell a ripe corn by its look,' Akoto remarked.

'Yes. My mission is to spread the word of God, so that all people will come to know Jesus Christ as their Lord and personal saviour,' the woman explained.

'Are you are an evangelist?' Akoto asked.

'Yes,' the woman replied.

'That is good. May God give you the strength to do the work of an evangelist to win more souls for Him. To do the work of God of any kind such as being an evangelist is the best work and the blessings associated with it are beyond measure,' Akoto asserted.

'Amen! Are you also an evangelist?' the woman inquired.

'No, but I'm a staunch Christian who has much concern for the work of God and I know that my association with you will promote my Christian life,' Akoto said.

'Amen! What work do you do?' the woman inquired.

'I'm a businessman. Can I have your phone number so that I can call you when something about the word of God bothers me?' Akoto requested.

The woman, who was a bit hesitant, gave her phone number to Akoto in exchange for his.

'May I also know your name?' Akoto requested.

'I'm called Ama.

'I'm called Akoto. Where do you live?' Akoto inquired.

'Pimso,' answered Ama.

'As a businessman, I have many friends who are businessmen in Pimso. Are you going there right now?' Akoto ascertained.

'Yes; I'm going to the station to take a car,' Ama explained.

'May God be with you and have a successful journey,' said Akoto.

'Amen!' Ama shouted hilariously.

When Akoto went home and was lying on his bed, he began to think.

'I can see that Ama is God fearing and a woman of noble character. I'll marry her if she has no husband. I must be tactful and diplomatic in dealing with her. I'll always use Christian jargons when I'm talking with her to make her believe that I'm a Christian.'

When three days had passed, Akoto called Ama on the phone.

'Who is calling?' Ama yelled when she received the phone call.

'It is Akoto, the young man you met three days ago on the street of Ankaasi. Have you forgotten about it?' Akoto asserted.

'Yes. Is it Mr. Akoto?' replied Ama.

'Yes. I'm calling you to inquire of your wellbeing,' said Akoto.

'I'm fine,' Ama enthused.

'We thank God. I'm also fine,' Akoto asserted.

'Thanks for calling,' Ama said.

'Thanks belong to God,' Akoto retorted.

'Next month, our church is organizing a seven-day evangelism crusade and I'm happy to invite you to it,' Ama requested.

'That is good. If God willing, I'll come to tap some of the anointing,' Akoto enthused.

'Amen! The anointing will overflow,' Ama shouted.

To the surprise of Ama, Akoto went to the evangelism crusade during which the church had many new converts.

'This crusade has helped me understand that Jesus Christ is the only saviour of the world through whom one can go to heaven. Therefore, I've agreed to worship Him as my Lord and personal saviour in truth and in spirit. May He help me to do it,' a new convert testified.

'Today, my joy knows no bounds because I have discovered the way to heaven and that way is Jesus Christ,' another new convert testified.

'I've a lot of money, properties and fame if I'm not boasting, but all these things are useless if it is not accompanied by my going to heaven, Therefore, I take Jesus Christ as my Lord and personal saviour through whom I will go to heaven,' another new convert also testified.

When it was the time for offertory, most of the congregation went to deposit money in the offertory box amid singing and dancing. Akoto, who was sitting at the back of the congregation, also went to deposit money in the offertory box amid singing and dancing. When he was in front of the congregation, he put his dancing styles and skills into action which held most of the congregation, including Ama spellbound. As he skillfully made forth and back movements amid jumping as part of his dancing styles, most of the congregation fixed their eyes on him because they were enthralled by his dancing.

CHAPTER THREE

As time went by, Akoto and Ama became friends. Akoto always maintained Christian composure in order to impress Ama. He often visited Ama to inquire of her wellbeing. Akoto, who was in love with Ama, sought an occasion to make amorous advances towards her, but there was no way. However, when they had been in friendship for two years, Akoto whose love for Ama had reached its pinnacle decided to make a marriage proposal to her.

'There are three major stages in the life of man which are birth, marriage and death,' Akoto asserted.

'Surely,' Ama interrupted.

'Without marriage, there will be no birth and human society will be no more. For this reason, it is important for every human being to have a wife or a husband,' Akoto explained.

Ama nodded in agreement as Akoto discussed marriage issues with her.

'Yes. What you are saying is true. The importance of marriage cannot be overemphasized,' Ama retorted.

'Genesis 2:24...*a man will leave his father and mother and be united to his wife, and they will become one flesh.* Ama, to fulfill this divine order, I want to marry a woman like you,' said Akoto.

'I don't understand you. What are you implying?' Ama retorted.

'I'm implying marriage,' Akoto explained.

Marriage? To whom?' Ama exclaimed.

'I'm in love with you, so I want to marry you,' Akoto explained.

'Ha-ha-ha-a!' Ama yelled.

'Why are you laughing?' Akoto interrupted.

'Are you not mistaken in your love?' asked Ama.

'No. My love for you is genuine; it is not a mistaken love,' Akoto explained.

'Are you sure?' asked Ama.

'Yes,' answered Akoto.

'What shows?' Ama demanded.

'Words alone cannot prove it. Actions, they say, speak louder than words,' Akoto replied.

'Then I've not seen your love for me in your actions. Have I been blind?' Ama retorted.

'No. You have not been blind. It may be that you haven't taken notice of my love for you expressed in my actions. It is not all people who are good at understanding body language,' Akoto explained.

'Anyway, have you prayed about your decision to marry me?' Ama asked.

'Specifically no, but generally yes,' answered Akoto.

'I don't understand what you mean by the statement; specifically no, but generally yes. May you clarify it?' Ama demanded.

'The statement means that I've not prayed about you for marriage, but I've been praying for God to help me choose a good wife and that wife in my observation is you,' Akoto explained.

'Ha-ha-ha-a! You will kill me with laughter. I'll like to suggest to you to pray about me if you really want to marry me because in my opinion and observation, I can't be your wife,' Ama asserted.

'Why?' asked Akoto.

'To answer it is to hurt your feelings and make you unhappy,' Ama explained.

'My love for you insofar as it is genuine has made me immune to being hurt by your words and therefore, I can absorb any word you tell me no matter how offensive it is,' Akoto remarked.

'We are incompatible,' Ama said.

'We are incompatible in what sense?' Akoto demanded.

'Are you born-again?' asked Ama.

'You need not ask me this question. I expect you to know the answer,' Akoto replied.

'I don't know the answer, so you must tell me,' Ama demanded.

'Don't you know what constitutes being born-again?' Akoto retorted.

'I know, but I can't tell whether you are born-again,' Ama explained.

'I'm born-again,' said Akoto.

'When did you become born-again?' Ama inquired.

'Why are all these questions? Do they have relevance to the subject matter of our discussion?' Akoto snarled.

'Yes, so you should answer them,' Ama replied.

'I became born-again two years ago,' Akoto said impetuously.

'Is it when you met me for the first time or after you met me?' asked Ama.

'Before I met you,' Akoto answered.

'Have you been baptized?' Ama inquired.

'Yes,' Akoto answered.

'In what church were you baptized?' Ama asked.

'Gateway Church,' Akoto stammered.

'What pastor baptized you?' Ama inquired.

'Pastor Arhin,' answered Akoto.

'Do you have a baptismal certificate?' Ama inquired.

'Why is this question? Does having a baptismal certificate make one born-again?' Akoto asked.

'No, but I need an answer,' replied Ama.

'I don't have a baptismal certificate,' Akoto said.

'Why is it that you have been baptized, but don't have a baptismal certificate?' Ama asked.

'I've not gone for it,' explained Akoto.

'I suggest you go for it,' Ama asserted.

'The pastor who baptized me has been transferred,' Akoto retorted.

'To say this is to make me doubt your trustworthiness and I can't marry someone whom I can't trust,' Ama muttered.

'To erase any doubt concerning my baptismal certificate, I will go for it,' Akoto said.

'It is up to you,' Ama retorted.

CHAPTER FOUR

When Akoto went home after the conversation, he confided in his friend, Asamoah, his intention to marry Ama.

'Coming to me this morning suggests that you have a serious matter to discuss with me,' Asamoah remarked.

'Yes. Your guess is correct,' Akoto said.

'What is it?' Asamoah demanded.

'I've seen a woman whom I have fallen in love with, but my attempts to woo her have proved futile,' said Akoto.

'You of all people, you couldn't woo her. What happened?' Asamoah asked with surprise.

'The woman is a staunch Christian who strictly adheres to the teachings of the Bible,' Akoto explained.

'How did you get to know her?' asked Asamoah.

'I've been in friendship with her for two years,' Akoto explained.

'For two years?' exclaimed Asamoah.

'Yes,' Akoto affirmed.

'Then you are smart,' Asamoah remarked.

'Yes, but my smartness has yielded no results,' Akoto retorted.

'What should I do for you?' Asamoah demanded.

'I want you to help me devise means to woo her,' said Akoto.

'You must control your emotions. You will succeed in wooing her because you have come to an expert in the field of relationships,' Asamoah said boastfully.

'I believe in you because none of your plans you have given me to woo women for the past years have failed and I know that this one will be no exception,' Akoto asserted.

'What is the woman's name?' asked Asamoah.

'Ama,' Akoto answered.

'Is she rich?' Asamoah inquired.

'No,' Akoto answered.

'Are the parents rich?' asked Asamoah.

'No,' Asamoah replied.

'Does she have a car?' Asamoah inquired.

'No,' answered Akoto.

'Good! Shake my hand. You are half-way successful,' said Asamoah.

'In what way?' Akoto demanded.

'Since she is not rich, enticing her with money will change her mind. Since most women are materialistic, buying her a posh car will make her change her mind and accept your marriage proposal,' Asamoah suggested.

'There are many ways to kill a cat. I'll try this suggestion and I hope it will work successfully,' Akoto asserted.

'Do you love the woman to extent of marrying her?' Asamoah inquired.

'Yes. If she accepts my proposal, I'll marry her,' Akoto replied.

'When you buy her the car to win her love and marry her, the car will still come back to you since she is your wife, so go and do my suggestion and you will come to congratulate me,' Asamoah explained.

'So be it,' Akoto remarked and went home. On arriving home, Akoto reclined in an armchair and began to cogitate.

'Asamoah's plan will work because every woman likes money. Since Ama is not rich, enticing her with money and gifts will make her love me and accept my proposal. This method has worked for many men and it will also work for me.'

Two months later, Akoto bought a brand-new car which was of high quality and presented it to Ama as a gift, all in an attempt to win her love. Ama was sitting on a chair in front of her house and was reading her Bible when Akoto went there. She was shocked to see Akoto alighting from the car, so she immediately closed her Bible to welcome him.

'Let's go inside,' she said.

'No. Let's sit here. There is enough shade here and the weather condition is favourable,' Akoto retorted.

Ama rushed to the house to pick up a chair for Akoto. When Akoto was seated, he inserted his right hand into his pocket and took a handkerchief to wipe his face.

'Ah! I'm tired,' he remarked.

'Let's pray,' Ama said and closed her eyes and held Akoto's hands.

'Oh God! I thank you that you have brought my guest to me successfully. Let our discussions be fruitful according to your will, Amen.'

'Amen!' Akoto responded.

'There is no way to know what is in a person's mind unless he tells you,' said Ama.

'Yes,' Akoto interrupted.

'What brings you here this morning?' Ama demanded.

Akoto cleared his throat and began to speak.

'As the rain water does not wash away the spots on a leopard, misunderstandings between us cannot wipe away my concern for you. Without more ado, it interests me to give you this envelope and the content is what I've decided to give you,' said Akoto.

'What is in the envelope?' Ama inquired while she collected it.

'Words alone cannot tell it,' Akoto retorted.

'Are you sure?' asked Ama.

'Yes,' answered Akoto.

When Ama, who was eager to know what is in the envelope, opened it she found car keys in it.

'What are these car keys for?' she asked with surprise.

'They are for you,' answered Akoto.

'For me?' Ama exclaimed.

'Yes,' Akoto affirmed.

'Do I own a car?' Ama asked.

'Yes,' replied Akoto.

'Ha-ha-ha-a! Are you speaking in riddles?' Ama exclaimed.

'No. I'm speaking in a plain language,' Akoto said.

'I don't seem to understand you. May you further explain what you mean?' Ama suggested.

'The car is for you,' Akoto asserted.

'What car?' Ama inquired.

'The one there,' Akoto said while he pointed out his right hand towards the car.

'Wow! This is surprising,' Ama exclaimed.

'This shouldn't be a surprise,' Akoto said.

'Are you giving the car to me as an act of generosity in the name of the Lord or in the name of mistaken love?' Ama asked.

'As an act of generosity in the name of the Lord, but anything including love which is mistaken can be corrected,' Akoto retorted.

'It is written in James 1:27 that *religion that God our Father accepts as pure and faultless is this: to look after orphans and widows in their distress and to keep oneself from being polluted by the world.* On this note, I suggest you sell the car and use the proceeds to take care of orphans and widows in their distress in order to increase your reward in heaven if going to heaven is your primary aim,' Ama said and threw the car keys back to Akoto.

'Ama, why is this attitude? You must calm down and reconsider your decision to repudiate my gift. My gift is a demonstration of generosity and concern,' Akoto snapped.

'I don't need a car now,' Ama retorted and went to the house while Akoto stood there disappointed and worried. Since Ama had refused to collect the car, he had no option than to drive the car back home.

CHAPTER FIVE

On the following day, Akoto went to Asamoah who was watching a movie at the time of his arrival, but the moment he saw Akoto, he stopped watching the movie and attended to him.

'I hope you've been victorious in winning Ama's love,' Asamoah asserted.

'The plan has backfired,' said Akoto.

'Backfired?' Asamoah shrieked.

'Yes,' Akoto affirmed.

'Why? What happened?' Asamoah inquired.

'She has refused to take the car I bought for her,' Akoto mumbled.

'This is uncommon. Did you ask her why she refused to take the car?' Asamoah inquired.

'She said I should sell the car and use the proceeds to take care of orphans and widows in their distress in order to increase my reward in heaven. She explained that to do so is a demonstration of pure religion that God accepts,' Akoto explained.

'How did you present the car to her? Did you show her the car?' Asamoah inquired.

'Yes, I did,' Akoto answered.

'Did you give the car keys to her to prove to her that you were truly willing to give the car to her?' Asamoah inquired.

'Yes,' replied Akoto.

'What was her reaction?' Asamoah demanded.

'She threw the car keys back to me and said, "she doesn't need a car,"' Akoto retorted.

'Don't be discouraged. Some women are like that. She just wants to show that she is not morally loose and that it is not easy to win her love,' Asamoah asserted.

'So what should I do?' Akoto inquired.

'Do you know any of her friends?' Asamoah asked.

Yes,' replied Akoto.

'Do the friends know that you are her friend?' Asamoah inquired.

'Yes,' answered Akoto.

'Then you can use the friends as an instrument to persuade her to accept your proposal. Different situations demand different strategies,' Asamoah suggested.

Akoto nodded in agreement and shook hands with Asamoah.

'This plan is good and it can work. I'll try it,' Akoto asserted.

'I want you to accompany me to a certain man who wants to sell a piece of land to me,' Asamoah requested.

'Do you want to build another house?' Akoto inquired.

Yes. I want to build a house for my parents who live in a rented house. They are aging and they must have a comfortable house to live in,' Asamoah explained.

'It is a good idea. Let's go,' Akoto ordered.

'Wait for me for a while. I want to change my shirt,' Asamoah said and went to the room and came back in three minutes time.

'Let's go,' he ordered.

As Asamoah and Akoto walked on the streets to the place, they talked about Ama.

'Ama wants to prove that she is a holy Christian who doesn't want to associate herself with a pagan by means of marriage,' Asamoah said.

'Ama hasn't seen that I'm a pagan; she knows that I'm a genuine Christian,' Akoto retorted.

'How come?' asked Asamoah.

'I've shown it by my actions that I'm indeed a Christian and she has believed it. I attend the same church with her and use Christian jargons whenever I'm talking with her,' Akoto explained.

'Do you know any quotations in the Bible?' Asamoah asked humorously.

'Don't mention it. I'm now a Bible scholar because of Ama. Sometimes, before I go to her, I memorize a Bible quotation which I say to impress her,' explained Akoto.

'Different situations demand different strategies, so you are adopting the strategy of hypocrisy to deal with Ama,' Asamoah shrieked.

'Exactly!' Akoto exclaimed.

'Then you will win her love,' Asamoah remarked.

'It is a surety,' Akoto retorted.

While Asamoah and Akoto were walking on the street, they reached a T-junction and took to the right road which led to the landowner's house. There was a white dog at the entrance of the landowner's house which barked as soon as it saw them entering the house. The dog's barking woke up the landowner who was asleep and made him think that someone had come to the house, so he rushed to the entrance of the house and beckoned to it to go to him when he saw Asamoah and Akoto at the entrance.

'My pet, keep mute and come to me,' he said while he beckoned to the dog.

When the dog heard his voice, it ran to lie down before him and kept quiet and he massaged it as an expression of admiration. Asamoah and Akoto, who were standing motionless at the entrance because they were frightened by the dog's barking, entered the house. When they were seated, the landowner asked their mission.

'It interests me to ask you your mission to my house at this time of the day,' the landowner asserted.

'You've asked well. I'm here to discuss with you the land I want to buy from you,' Asamoah said succinctly.

'That is good. I've finished preparing the documents of the land. Yesterday, I had a discussion with the lawyers and they said the documents are ready, so you must pay the full royalty of the land,' the landowner explained.

'The payment of the royalty is not a problem to me. What matters is the documents,' Asamoah retorted.

'When are you going to make full payment of the royalty?' the landowner inquired.

'When the documents are available,' replied Asamoah.

'Tomorrow, I'll go for them from the lawyers so Friday, come for them,' said the landowner.

'When I come on Friday, I will make full payment of the royalty so you should not disappoint me,' Akoto asserted.

On the following day, the landowner went to collect the documents of the land from the lawyers who had prepared them and when Akoto had paid the full royalty, he gave the documents to him.

Without delay, Akoto hired workers to prepare the land for building construction. Thus, the land was cleared and marked out for building a house. Masons who were employed put their expertise and wide range of knowledge of building construction into action to build the house.

Within eight months, the masons had put up a magnificent house for Asamoah which attracted people to buy it, but Asamoah did not sell it to any of them.

'I've built this house for my parents who are aging, but have no good house to stay in, so I'll not sell it or rent it out to people,' Asamoah always told people.

CHAPTER SIX

One morning, Akoto went to Abena, Ama's friend.

'Good morning,' Akoto greeted.

'Good morning,' responded Abena.

'How are you?' asked Akoto.

'I'm doing well,' answered Abena.

'We thank God,' Akoto remarked.

'I've not been seeing you nowadays,' Abena said.

'Yes. Too much business activities have not permitted me to visit friends nowadays which I know is a bad attitude,' Akoto explained.

'You shouldn't burden yourself with too much business activities. You must have enough leisure. It is said all work and no play makes Jack a dull boy,' said Abena.

'From today, I'll find time to pay you visits,' Akoto retorted.

'May I know the message you have for me which underpins your coming here?' Abena demanded.

'Two heads are better than one. There is something which is of grave concern to me that I want to discuss with you because I can't deal with it alone and whether or not it is good for me to tell you is left to judgment,' said Akoto.

'You can tell me anything which worries you. Maybe, I can help you,' Abena asserted.

'There is a flower in a garden which is so beautiful and dear to my heart that I want to pluck it, but I can't do so without seeking advice and directions from you because it maybe that the flower is not worth plucking,' Akoto remarked.

'A flower?' Abena asked with surprise.

'Yes, a flower,' Akoto affirmed.

'Are you speaking in riddles?' 'Your statement beats my comprehension. Can you explain it better?' Abena requested.

'The flower I'm talking about is Ama, your friend,' Akoto explained.

'Do we pluck a human being?' Abena asked with surprise.

'Ha-ha-ha-a! I now know that you don't understand riddles,' Akoto retorted.

'Why are you laughing? You must answer my question,' Abena insisted.

'The statement means to ask for Ama's hand in marriage from her parents,' explained Akoto.

'Do you mean that you want to marry Ama?' Abena asked.

'Surely,' answered Akoto.

'Have you told her something about your decision to marry her?' Abena inquired.

'Yes,' replied Akoto.

'What did she say?' Abena demanded.

'She debunked my marriage proposal,' Akoto answered.

'Then what do you want me to do in connection with your marriage plans?' Abena demanded.

'Ama thinks that I'm not serious and that I'm flattering her with a frivolous proposal, so I entreat you to tell her something on my behalf. In that way, she will know that I'm serious to marry her and she will take my words seriously,' Akoto suggested.

'Do you think I can force Ama to love and marry you?' asked Abena.

'You can't force her to love and marry me, but as your friend, you can tell her to do the right thing and make informed choices, including choosing a marriage partner. As a Christian man, it is in the right direction to be paired with a Christian woman in marriage and to tell you to help me in asking for Ama's hand in marriage is not wrong,' Akoto explained.

'How many times have you made proposals to Ama,' Abena inquired.

'Only once, but I've now realized that for me to do that was a deviation from the word of God. Thus, I've decided to use Christian procedures to ask for her hand in marriage. Abena, your success in talking to Ama on my behalf will not go unrewarded. I don't say much but I do much,' Akoto asserted.

'Are you sure that my success in talking to Ama on your behalf will be rewarded? Abena asked.

'Yes,' replied Akoto.

'Do you want to bribe me to talk to Ama on your behalf?' Abena asked.

'No. To show appreciation or give you a reward for doing something good for me is not a bribe,' explained Akoto.

'I don't think I can talk to Ama to accept your proposal. I'll only advice you to persist in your proposal. Maybe, she will change her mind with time,' Abena retorted.

'To say this is to discourage me,' Akoto snarled.

'This is not a discouragement,' Abena remarked.

'Abena, you are the only person who can help me in this situation,' Akoto mumbled.

'I'm very sorry that I can't help you in this situation. I can't tell Ama to love you,' Abena explained.

'Do you say this to deter me from giving you the reward that I have for you?' Akoto asserted.

'What reward do you have for me?' Abena asked.

'This is what I have for you,' Akoto said while he handed an envelope to Abena.

'What is it? Is it a letter you want me to give to Ama?' Abena inquired.

'No. It is for you,' replied Akoto.

'For me?' Abena exclaimed.

'Yes,' Akoto answered.

'What is in it?' Abena inquired.

'To say it is to boast. May you see it for yourself?' Akoto suggested.

When Abena opened the envelope, she was shocked to see a cheque in it.

'What is this cheque for?' Abena inquired.

'It is for you. Take it to Success Bank and cash it,' Akoto ordered.

'Wow! The amount is quite substantial,' Abena enthused.

'This is small. There are better things you will have if you do the assignment,' Akoto asserted.

'Are you sure?' Abena asked.

'Yes. It will not surprise you that your success in accomplishing the assignment will see you driving in one of the posh cars,' Akoto asserted.

'Eh! Then I'll be rich,' Abena exclaimed.

'You will be rich if you decide to be rich because riches are near you. It is up to you to grab it or let it elude you,' said Akoto.

'Wow! You must leave everything for me. I know how I will talk to Ama to accept your proposal,' Abena said.

Having held thorough discussions with Abena, Akoto went home with a high sense of assurance that he will win Ama's love through Abena. On the next day, when it was 10:00am, Abena dressed gorgeously and went to cash the cheque from the bank.

When five days had passed, Abena went to Ama in the house at the time she was reading a Bible. Ama who was filled with much joy hurried to hug her upon seeing her.

'I've missed you so much. Did you travel?' she remarked.

'No,' Abena retorted.

'Then why have I not been seeing you for the past seven days?' Ama asked.

'I'm always in the house for the reason that I don't want my creditors to see me often,' Abena explained.

'God will help you pay your debts. How is your business?' Ama asserted.

'Of late, it is declining; many customers do not come to buy things and I don't understand it,' Abena muttered.

'You must have faith in God regardless of the situation. God will change the situation and you will have more customers and your business will blossom,' Ama said.

'So be it,' Abena retorted.

'Nothing comes easy. Therefore, I'll encourage you to persist in prayers,' Ama suggested.

'How can you pray effectively if you have problems and don't have a sound mind,' Abena complained.

'To say this is wrong. The word of God admonishes us to pray without ceasing. This implies that you must pray effectively when you have problems and when you don't have problems. Don't allow your problems to overshadow you,' explained Ama.

Abena then laid bare the main purpose of going to Ama.

'Ama, I'll like to discuss an issue with you which can antagonize you. However, may you give me the permission to discuss it with you since it can bring good results,' Abena said.

'Wisdom is not in the head of one person. If you have advice which can bring me something good, why should you hesitate to tell me whether or not it may offend me? For me to refuse to take your advice does not mean that it is not good. It may be that it does not suit my interest,' Ama explained.

'The issues of love and marriage cannot be downplayed. Thus, it is necessary for everyone whether great or small to have a spouse at a certain stage of life unless one decides to remain unmarried,' Abena said.

'Have you got a suitor?' Ama interrupted sharply.

'No. You must not rush into knowing what I want to tell you. May you exercise patience and be all ears,' Ama suggested.

'Then you must continue your speech,' Abena ordered.

'In my opinion, I'll say that the man who has made a marriage proposal to you is the right person to marry,' Abena asserted.

'What man?' asked Ama.

'Akoto,' Abena replied.

'Who told you that Akoto wants to marry me,' Ama inquired.

'Every serious and God-fearing man who wants to marry a woman does not court her in secret and in darkness. Thus, I think it is not wrong for Akoto to tell me his decision to marry you. This shows his seriousness and good Christian culture,' Abena retorted.

'Do you mean that it is Akoto who told you that he wants to marry me?' Ama asked.

'Yes,' answered Abena.

'And what did you tell him?' Ama inquired.

'I told him that it is a good idea for two staunch Christians to marry,' Abena replied.

'Who told you that Akoto is a Christian?' Ama asked.

'Why are you asking me this question? Don't you know Akoto? Don't you attend the same church with him?' Abena mumbled.

'Attending the same church with someone doesn't make the person a Christian. The truth is that Akoto is not a Christian,' Ama explained.

'Why do you say this? For someone like you to say that Akoto is not a Christian is a lie. I know Akoto to be a committed Christian. Hardly does he absent himself from church activities,' Abena argued.

'You have been deceived by his outward appearance. All that glitters is not gold,' Ama remarked.

'Why are you using derogatory words to describe Akoto? It is your wrong perception about him that has made you use those words to describe him,' Abena snarled.

'I can't marry Akoto,' Ama said.

'Ama, you are aging and therefore, you must settle down with a husband. Nowadays, it is not easy to have a well-to-do and God-fearing man like Akoto to marry.

Postponing your marriage by rejecting men who could be your husband will not augur well for you,' Abena explained.

'I'm fervently praying for a husband and I know that at the appointed time, God will help me get one,' Ama said.

'Now is the appointed time. Akoto is suitable for you, so you must not be reluctant to marry him. It is said make hay while the sun shines,' Abena asserted.

'How can I marry a man I don't know the work that he does?' Ama muttered.

'Don't you know that Akoto is a businessman?' asked Abena.

'What business does he do?' Ama demanded.

'Has he not told you that he deals in the importation of televisions and computers,' Abena remarked.

'This is what he says,' Ama asserted.

'Then why are you saying that you don't know the work that he does? You see! You have no tangible reason to say that Akoto cannot be a good husband to you,' said Abena.

'I'm praying about him and if it is the will of God to marry him, I'll do so,' Ama explained.

'You should not be too selective. Akoto is okay for you as a husband; he has money and can take good care of you when you marry him,' Abena explained.

'Money is not the only yardstick to consider when choosing a spouse. There are other factors that should be considered,' Ama remarked.

'Akoto is in love with you, so he will not treat you badly if you marry him. You must reciprocate his love for you by agreeing to marry him,' Abena retorted.

'The devil is using marriage as a means to enslave some people and I don't want to fall victim. This explains why divorce has become common among many people, including some Christians,' Ama explained.

'What you are saying is true, but as a Christian you must believe that with God in your marriage, the devil can't use it as a means to enslave you,' said Abena.

'I'll think about your advice as to whether I should marry Akoto,' Ama suggested.

'To refuse to marry Akoto is to delay your marriage because he is the right man for you. You are now twenty-eight and when do you want to marry? Do you want to marry at an old age? You must consider these questions well and act in accordance with them,' Abena asserted.

'There is no delay in the sight of God. The so-called delay in the sight of God is quickness and success in disguise,' explained Ama.

When Abena had gone home after the discussion, Ama went to lie supine on her bed and folded her arms and started thinking.

'In my opinion and observation, Akoto is not the right man for me. Why should I marry him? He is not trustworthy. Won't he give me severe problems if I marry him? Nonetheless, he has money and can take good care of me. He is the sixth person who has proposed to me and I have disagreed. Should I marry him or continue to make a search for a man who meets my requirements?'

CHAPTER SEVEN

Three days later, Akoto went to Abena to find out whether she had been able to influence Ama to marry him.

'Have you talked to Ama?' Akoto inquired.

'Yes,' replied Abena.

'What did she say?' Akoto demanded.

'She said she is thinking about it,' answered Abena.

'Do you think she will change her mind and marry me?' Akoto asked.

'Surely. I've made her understand the need to marry you. She will by all means agree to marry you, so you must be thinking about how you are going to organize your wedding,' Abena said.

'The wedding is not a problem. You know that I've money to organize any type of wedding no matter how expensive it will cost. I'll say it again that your success in making Ama marry me will not go unrewarded. It will see you driving in one of the posh cars,' Akoto said.

'Are you not flattering me?' asked Abena.

'Your success will tell,' Akoto said while he unzipped his wallet to take money from it and gave it to Abena.

'Take this money to buy something,' he remarked.

'Wow! Your decision to marry Ama will soon crystallize,' Abena asserted.

Akoto went home with much assurance that Ama would agree to marry him. When two weeks had passed, Abena confronted Ama again for another discussion.

'I believe that you have finished making the right decision which will mark a new chapter in your life,' Abena asserted.

'What right decision?' Ama interrupted abruptly.

'A decision which will change your status as a spinster to a bride,' Abena said.

'I've finished making that decision,' Ama remarked.

'Then very soon, you will be addressed Mrs. Akoto,' Abena enthused.

'What?' Mrs. Akoto? No. I'm no longer thinking about him because I will not marry him,' explained Ama.

'Ama, you must have second thoughts to marry Akoto. He is not only a Christian, but also a well-to-do man who will be responsible and tender you with love. What sort of man do you want to marry?' Abena snarled.

'God will provide. Akoto and I are incompatible,' Ama retorted.

'In what way?' Abena asked.

'Careful studies about him show that he is a wolf in sheep's clothing. I want to marry someone who is heavenly minded,' Ama explained.

'When will you stop having wrong perceptions about Akoto? You must disabuse your mind of the wrong perceptions you have about him and make an informed decision,' Abena suggested.

'I can't change my decision. To tell me to marry Akoto is tantamount to building castles in the air; it is an impossible task,' Ama retorted.

As days went by, Abena did all that she could to coax Ama into marrying Akoto, but her efforts were in vain.

'I've talked to Ama at length to make her convinced to marry you, but she is adamant. Therefore, you should quit her and look for another woman and I know that you can have someone as good as Ama or even better than her,' Abena suggested.

'For me to quit Ama is painful like plucking the hairs in my nose. I know that you have done what you can, but I will still press on to win her love,' Akoto mumbled.

One day, Akoto informed his uncle and other elderly men to inform Ama's parents about his decision to marry her. Akoto had the idea that with the influence and intervention of Ama's parents, he would succeed in his plans to marry her.

'I'll let some elderly men go to Ama's parents to ask for her hand in marriage for me. In that way, the parents will know that I'm serious and a responsible man and they can make her change her mind and marry me,' Akoto thought.

Accordingly, one evening, at 4:00, Akoto and his uncle and other elderly men went to Ama's parents to have a discourse with them.

'My nephew who does not want to woo your daughter in secret and in darkness has expressed the desire to marry her, but he can't do so without toeing the line of custom. Thus, our presence here is to ask for your daughter's hand in marriage for him,' Akoto's uncle said laconically.

'I've two daughters. Which one?' Ama's father asked.

'Ama,' answered Akoto's uncle.

'Where is your nephew?' Ama's father inquired.

'Here is he,' Akoto's uncle said as he pointed his right hand at Akoto who was sitting beside him.

'What is his name?' Ama's father asked.

'He is called Akoto,' the uncle replied.

'Akoto, may I know the work that you do?' asked Ama's father.

'I'm a businessman who deals in the importation of televisions and computers,' answered Akoto.

'What is your religious affiliation?' Ama's father asked.

'I'm a Christian who worships at Gateway Church,' Akoto replied.

'Oh nice! We are also members of Gateway Church. My wife and I are pleased that you have come to ask for Ama's hand in marriage, but we can't accept your marriage proposal without first seeking her consent. Therefore, we beseech you to go and come next month for a reply,' Ama's father explained.

'We thank you for your enthusiastic reception and inspiring words,' Akoto uncle's asserted.

When Akoto and his retinue had left the place for their homes,' Ama's father and mother talked about Akoto.

'Ama's suitor may have money,' the father said.

'How do you know?' the mother asked.

'I've learned that businessmen who are importers have money and Ama's suitor will be no exception,' the father explained.

'If he has money, then we are blessed. If our son-in-law has money, we can be better off,' the mother remarked.

'That is what we expect,' the father retorted.

On the next day, in the morning, when Ama had finished doing her household chores, the mother went to her in her house.

'Your coming to me at this time without calling me on the phone shows that something serious is at stake,' Ama remarked.

'I'm here to pay you a visit because I've not seen you for days,' the mother explained.

'Thank you,' Ama retorted.

'How is your clothing business?' the mother inquired.

'It is booming,' answered Ama.

'We thank God,' said the mother.

'Is dad at home now?' Ama inquired.

'No. He has gone to farm. He'll need you this evening,' the mother asserted.

'Has anything serious happened?' Ama inquired.

'No. He has an important issue to discuss with you,' the mother explained.

'I'll do well to come,' Ama remarked.

'Then we will be expecting you,' the mother said and asked permission to go home.

In the evening, Ama, after taking her supper, dressed decently and rushed to the father. By the time she went to the father; he was already seated and was waiting for her.

'Dad, good evening,' Ama greeted.

'Good evening my daughter,' the father responded.

'Mum came to tell me in the morning that you need me urgently. I've come to hear the message you have for me,' Ama asserted.

'I have an important issue to discuss with you and your mother must be part of the discussion, so go and call her in the room,' the father ordered.

Ama, without delay, went to call the mother.

'Mum, dad needs you at the meeting,' Ama said.

When Ama and the mother were seated for the meeting, the father began to talk.

'Ama, it is a delight to have this meeting with you. A certain young man who is enamored of you has come to us with his relatives to ask for your hand in marriage.'

'What is the man's name?' Ama cut in.

'Akoto,' the father replied.

'I'll not marry him,' Ama mumbled.

'Why do you say this?' Do you know him?' the father asked.

'Yes,' replied Ama.

'Ama, don't be impetuous in saying this. A young man who does not want to woo you in secret and in darkness, but comes directly to your parents to ask for your hand in marriage is well mannered and God fearing who is worth marrying,' Ama's father explained.

'Akoto and I are not compatible. Therefore, I won't marry him,' Ama retorted.

'On what grounds? Is he not a Christian?' the father asked.

'He claims to be a Christian, but I don't see him as such,' explained Ama.

'Does he not attend church?' the father inquired.

'He does,' Ama replied.

'Then how are you not compatible?' the father demanded.

'It is not all those who attend church are Christians. 2 Corinthians 11:13-15; *for such men are false apostles, deceitful workmen, masquerading as apostles of Christ. And no wonder, for Satan himself masquerades as an angle of light. It is not surprising, then, if his servants masquerade as servants of righteousness...*' Ama explained.

'We can't force you to marry Akoto whom you claim is not suitable for you. However, we will advise you to think about his proposal to marry you as you go home,' the mother suggested.

As days went by, Ama's parents made background investigations about Akoto and they got to know that he does not only have money, but he was also a Christian. This made them convinced that he could be a good and responsible husband to Ama. Thus, they made efforts to influence her to marry him, but she did not yield to their influence.

'Ama, you must reconsider your decision not to marry Akoto. By our investigations, Akoto could be a good and responsible husband to you. He has money to take good care of you. You know that we are poor and your marriage to him can relieve us from financial problems. Some women who were once poor have become better off through their marriages and you can be one of them,' Ama's mother explained.

'Mum, to say this is to underrate the power of God to make us rich. Should I marry Akoto because he has money?' Ama said.

'No, but your marriage to him can be the means that God is using to bless you and your parents?' the mother retorted.

'It is undeniable that God can use marriage to bless me, but not my marriage to Akoto. I have the intuition that Akoto is a wolf in sheep's clothing and that he is not a good Christian,' Ama said.

'How true is your so-called intuition? Isn't it a mirage or a hallucination?' the mother shrieked.

'Whether or not my intuition is a mirage or a hallucination doesn't make me convinced to marry Akoto,' Ama retorted.

'Ama, don't be recalcitrant and refuse to take your parents' advice. What actually is your reason for refusing to marry Akoto?' the mother demanded.

'I've already told you that Akoto whom you want me to marry is a wolf in sheep's clothing and therefore, not a good Christian and I'll not marry someone like him,' Ama asserted.

'Is it mandatory for a Christian to marry only Christian?' the mother asked.

'Mum, I'm surprised by your question. 2 Corinthians 6:14-15; *do not be yoked together with unbelievers. For do righteousness and wickedness have in common? Or what fellowship can light have with darkness? What harmony is there between Christ and Belial? What does a believer have in common with an unbeliever?'* Ama quoted the scripture to answer the mother.

'Have you got a Christian who is well-do-do like Akoto to marry?' the mother inquired.

'No. I'm still waiting for God and I believe that He will help me get one,' said Ama.

'For how long will you wait for God?' the mother muttered.

'No one can fix time for God to suit his own whims and caprices,' Ama retorted.

'Ama, we are your parents and have a wide range of experiences in life, so we know what is good for you. We can't let you marry someone who is irresponsible and not suitable for you. You must marry Akoto,' the father intervened.

'Dad, to compel me to marry Akoto is to put a millstone around my neck,' Ama said.

'Hey! You must not talk to me like that. You must mind the choice of your words because I'm your father,' the father said snarled.

'Yes dad!' Ama exclaimed.

'Your elder sister who is now a divorcee didn't listen to our advice and did what you are doing only to marry an irresponsible man who has divorced her. Do you also want to marry an irresponsible man who will create problems for you?' the father snarled.

'Dad, why do you say that I'm going to marry an irresponsible man?' asked Ama.

'Your attitude shows,' the father explained.

'I know that at the appointed time God will help me get a husband of my heart,' Ama remarked.

'This is the appointed time. God will not directly bring a husband to you. God works through people like your parents. Akoto can be your God-given husband and you must marry him,' the father asserted.

'Dad, how do you know?' Do you have proof?' Ama asked.

'Don't you know that I can also have an intuition?' the father retorted.

'Let us exercise patience in the Lord and wait to see what the future will be,' Ama suggested.

'Up to when should we exercise patience and wait?' You must not linger to marry Akoto. The devil knows that when you marry him, you will enjoy peace and prosperity, so he wants to prevent you from marrying him and pair you with the wrong man,' the father explained.

'It takes the word of God and prayers to overcome the devil and his schemes,' Ama retorted.

After a month, Akoto and his uncle and other elderly men went to Ama's parents again for feedback on Akoto's decision to marry her.

'Good morning,' greeted Akoto's uncle.

'Good morning,' Ama's parents responded in unison.

'A month ago, we came here to seek Ama's hand in marriage for my nephew. We have come for feedback,' Akoto's uncle said.

'Hmmm! Ama father sighed, 'I've talked to my daughter about Akoto's decision to marry her, but she is not interested in the marriage. Thus, I beseech Akoto to take it kindly. However, if she has a change of mind, I will notify you.'

Akoto whose face was downcast broke silence.

'It is quite usual for a woman to reject a man's offer of marriage at the initial stage, but I know that if it is the will of God for me to marry Ama, she will have a change of mind because no one can oppose the plans of God.'

The moment Akoto said this, Ama's mother nodded in understanding and remarked, 'Your words are inspiring and how I wish my daughter would marry a God-fearing man like you.'

Day in, day out, Ama's father and mother pestered her to agree to marry Akoto, but she did not.

'Do you know more than your parents?' the father mumbled.

'No,' replied Ama.

'Then why are you not agreeing to marry Akoto whom we have proof that he can take good care of you? Don't you know that your parents have the responsibility to give you to a man whom we approve in marriage?' the father remarked.

'Yes, but that man must be someone whom I love,' Ama retorted.

'What do you know about love? Do you want to teach me what love is? It is said you can't teach an old dog new tricks,' the father muttered.

'Don't you know that it is God who wants to bless you by allowing a Christian who has money to marry you, so that your parents will be better off? Do you want me and your father to die in poverty? You must reconsider your decision and tell us something positive,' the mother intervened.

'Mum, you will not die in poverty. Philippians 4:19 says *and my God shall supply all your need according to His riches in glory by Christ Jesus,*'Ama quoted from the New King James version of the Bible.

Akoto who was in love with Ama and was determined to marry her did not give up in making proposals to her, so one evening he went to have another discussion with her.

'Ama, when will our wedding ceremony and its solemnization take place,' Akoto said tactfully.

'I don't know,' Ama retorted.

'Then should I tell you?' Akoto asked.

'Yes,' replied Ama.

'Next month,' said Akoto.

'Next month?' asked Ama.

'Yes,' Akoto affirmed.

'Then you are deceiving yourself,' Ama said.

'Why?' asked Akoto.

'How can you wed a woman who has not agreed to marry you? Is it possible?' Ama asserted.

'That is why I'm here to make it possible,' Akoto said.

'In what way can you make it possible?' Ama inquired.

'Ama, I entreat you to calm down and consider the benefits of being married to a man like me who is prepared to tender you with love. Words are inadequate to express how I'm in love with you,' Akoto said lovingly.

'What benefits are you talking about?' Ama inquired.

'The benefits of true love, maximum care, comfort and peace which are ingredients of a stable and successful marriage,' explained Akoto.

'Ha-ha-ha-a! What you are saying is laughable?' Ama asserted.

'What makes it laughable?' Akoto demanded.

'Don't you know it yourself? Am I the only woman whom you can love?' Ama remarked.

'Yes,' answered Akoto, 'and love must be reciprocal.'

'Reciprocal? Then, not in my case,' Ama retorted.

'To say this is to make me die in my love for you,' Akoto muttered.

'To die for me in the name of mistaken love is stupidity. You must die for Christ. Apostle Peter and Stephen in the Bible died for Christ. This is the kind of dying I want you to die,' Ama explained.

'Are you insulting me?' asked Akoto.

'No. I'm telling you the truth. Any dying which is not accompanied by your going to heaven, no matter how great or small you are, is pathetic and therefore, can be said to be stupid,' Ama explained.

When it was evident to Akoto that Ama would not agree to marry him, he had no option than to coil into his shell and console himself with the thought that Ama would one day change her mind and agree to marry him. Accordingly, he no longer pestered her with marriage proposals.

CHAPTER EIGHT

As days went by, Asamoah came into contact with a woman, Esi, whom he became interested in. Asamoah saw Esi at a nightclub and approached her while she was dancing. He held her hands and danced with her. When the dancing was over, he engaged her in a conversation.

'You are good at dancing,' Asamoah said.

'Thank you,' Esi remarked.

'I'm Asamoah. May I know your name?' Asamoah asked.

'I'm Esi.

'Are you living in this city?' asked Asamoah.

'No. I'm living in Abenso,' Esi replied.

'That big city?' Asamoah remarked.

'Yes,' said Esi.

'Oh good! When are you going back to Abenso?' Asamoah inquired.

'Next three days,' replied Ama.

'Will it be a problem to you if I come to visit you there?' Asamoah inquired.

'No,' replied Esi.

'Then how do I get in touch with you? Can I have your phone number?' Asamoah requested.

'Of course,' Esi said and gave him her phone numbers and he typed them on his phone.

'All right, I'll call you when the need arises,' Asamoah asserted.

When Asamoah went home, he told Akoto about his new-found friend, Esi.

'I'm in the process of getting a wife,' said Asamoah.

'Is she in this city?' Akoto inquired.

'No,' answered Asamoah.

'Where does she live?' asked Akoto.

'Abenso,' answered Asamoah.

'How did you meet her?' Akoto inquired.

'I met her at a nightclub where I danced with her,' Asamoah explained.

'You must keep an eye on her before you enter into a relationship with her,' Akoto advised.

'Don't you trust me? Am I not experienced when it comes to relationships?' Asamaoh asserted.

With time, Asamoah and Esi became lovers.

'It interests me to say that you are lovable and worthy of being married,' Asamoah said.

'Thank you,' Esi enthused.

'Very soon, you will wear the wedding gown bought by me,' Asamoah said.

'Really?' Esi yelled and used her right hand to caress Asamoah's head.

'Do you really love me?' she asked while caressing Asamoah's head.

'Why do you doubt my love for you? Don't you trust my words?' Asamoah retorted.

'May my sweet love grant me favour to ask what I need urgently?' Esi requested while caressing Asamoah's head.

'Why can't my prospective wife ask what she needs from me?' Asamoah retorted.

'Thank you. My first request is that I want to introduce you to my parents, so that I will have confidence in you that you will marry me. After that, I'll tell you my second request,' Esi asserted.

'You are wise and well cultured to know what is required of your prospective husband. Desiring to introduce me to your parents is in the right direction and makes me believe that you are serious to marry me. For this reason, I promise to do your second request provided it is within my means,' Asamoah said lovingly.

'When are we going to my parents?' Esi demanded.

'Let's make it next month,' answered Asamoah.

'Please, don't disappoint me on that time because I will inform my parents of your decision to visit them,' Esi asserted.

'I'll fulfill my promise, so you must not anticipate disappointment,' Asamoah said.

On the first Saturday of the following month, Esi took Asamoah to see her parents in Abenso, but according to the mother, the father was not available; he had travelled.

Esi's mother was very happy to see Asamoah, her prospective son-in-law and gave him a warmest reception.

'I'm in high spirits to see my prospective son-in-law today. My daughter has spoken well of you and for you to come here gives credence to the good information I heard about you. Thus, I need no proof again that you are willing to marry my daughter and that you have no intention to deceive her,' Esi's mother said excitedly.

'I'm also elated to come to my prospective mother-in-law to see how she is faring. My coming here is to create the awareness that my willingness to marry your daughter is not in doubt and that I have no atom of doubt to deceive her,' Asamoah said.

Having had series of discussions with Esi's mother, Asamoah presented gifts to her after which he left for Pimso, leaving Esi behind. A week later, when Esi left the mother to go to Pimso, Asamoah also introduced her to his parents as his prospective wife and the parents had no choice than to accept his decision to marry her. However, Asamoah's parents asked him to allow them make thorough background investigations about Esi and her family, but Asamoah asked them to wait for the meantime until he gave them the permission to do so.

Now that Asamoah and Esi had known each other's parents, they had much confidence that their relationship would lead to marriage. One day, when they were discussing about how they would organize their wedding ceremony, Esi told Asamoah her second request.

'Sweetheart, can I tell you my second request that you have promised to do for me?' Esi said lovingly.

'Why not? Tell me what I should do for you. I've promised you of doing it if it is within my means,' Asamoah asserted.

'You know that I live in a dilapidated rented house and I'll be very happy if you build or buy a house for me so that I live there after our wedding. Your prospective wife and future children must have their own house,' Esi requested.

'Hmmm,' Asamoah sighed, 'your request is too high. However, I'll think about it.

Esi stood up from where she was sitting and went to sit on Asamoah's lap and started caressing him, especially the chin.

'Sweetheart, I know that it is costly to build or buy a house for me. However, if you consider the disadvantages of your wife and your future children living in a dilapidated rented house, it may not be wrong if you build or buy a house for me which implies building or buying a house for your children that I'll bear for you,' Esi said lovingly.

'Why don't we have the wedding before I build or buy you the house?' Asamoah suggested.

'Now, I don't have a good and comfortable place to stay and my rent is due. To avoid the hassles and the problems of staying in someone's house, I think having my own house will be much better,' Esi explained.

'It is not customarily right for me to provide a house for you while I've not married you. I don't understand why you want me to build or buy a house for you,' Asamoah muttered.

'To say this is to make me doubt your concern and love for me. Don't you have the means to build or buy the house?' Esi mumbled.

'I have, but I just don't understand why you are demanding a house before our wedding,' Asamoah snapped.

As they argued over the house issue, Asamoah, who was under the spell of love, finally agreed to provide the house for Esi.

'My love for you is not utopian and to demonstrate it is to say that you will have the house,' said Asamoah.

'Wow! Thank you,' Esi said while she knelt down before Asamoah to express her felicitations.

'Stand up! Asamoah ordered and held Esi's hands to help her get up.

'It does not only take money for a man to do this for his prospective wife, but also a true love,' Esi remarked.

'I've already built a house in the neighborhood of Maranatha that I've decided to give to my parents. I'll give it to you and build another one for them later,' Asamoah asserted.

'Have you built a house in the neighbourhood of Maranatha?' Esi asked with surprise.

'Yes,' replied Asamoah.

'Then you haven't told me. When did you build it?' asked Esi.

'Last year,' Asamoah answered.

'Then it is fashionable,' Esi remarked.

'Don't mention it,' Asamoah retorted.

'Really?' Esi yelled.

'Yes,' replied Asamoah.

'Ha-ha-ha-a! You have foresight,' Esi enthused.

'Tomorrow, at 4:00pm, I'll take you to the house to see it,' Asamoah suggested.

'Thank you,' Esi remarked.

To fulfill his promise, Asamoah took Esi to see the house and she liked it.

'Eh! Is this house for you?' It is exquisite,' Esi remarked with surprise.

'Yes,' Asamoah retorted.

'Then you are rich. I now believe that you are a man of substance,' Esi commended Asamoah.

'It is said a loaded wagon makes no noise. What you see explains how hard working I am and it is just a microcosm of what I want to do,' said Asamoah.

'Are you giving this house to me?' Esi asked with doubt.

'Yes,' replied Asamoah.

'Eh! To do this is uncommon and it tells the sort of man you are. There is every proof that your love for me is real,' Esi said.

Esi who was hilarious hugged Asamoah and kissed him on the cheeks.

'You are lovable, caring and kind,' she said romantically.

'Do you now believe that I'm trustworthy and that I do what I promise?' Asamoah asked.

'Yes but I want you to do something in connection with the house for me to make what you have done complete,' Esi requested.

'Is it within my means?' Asamoah inquired.

'Of course,' replied Esi.

'What is it?' Asamoah demanded.

'I beg you to prepare the documents of the house for me. This will make me believe you hundred percent that you have given it to me from the bottom of your heart,' Esi suggested.

'This is not a difficult thing to do. I'll prepare the documents of the house for you to prove that I've given it to you from the bottom of my heart,' said Asamoah.

As days went by, Asamoah prepared the documents of the house in the name of Esi. Accordingly, Esi who lived in a rented room moved to live in the house with much happiness and she enjoyed the comfort and serenity in the house. Asamoah who cared about her often went to her in the house. As their relationship progressed, they took a unanimous decision to legalize it; they planned to have a wedding. Rumors and issues about the wedding became the topics for discussion in every nook and cranny. While they had not fixed the time for the wedding, Asamoah informed the friends about it and invited them in advance to attend it.

'It is my singular pleasure to tell you that you must be prepared to attend my wedding which will come to light any moment from now,' Asamoah told the friends.

'Don't worry. We will endeavor to come to your wedding in numbers to grace it. We wish you the best of plans,' the friends retorted.

CHAPTER NINE

A month after Asamoah had given the house to Esi; he had broken-heartedness when he went to the house to know that Esi had moved from the house without his prior knowledge. He found a woman who was living in the house.

'Good morning,' greeted Asamoah.

'Good morning,' the woman responded.

'I'm looking for Esi,' said Asamoah.

'Who is Esi?' the woman inquired.

'The owner of this house,' Asamoah explained.

'I'm the owner of this house,' the woman retorted.

'The owner?' Asamoah exclaimed.

'Yes,' the woman affirmed.

'When did you become the owner of the house?' Asamoah inquired.

'Why are you asking me questions? Do you want to poke your nose into my private affairs?' the woman mumbled.

'I'm surprised to hear that you are the owner of the house because my prospective wife is the owner of this house,' Asamoah explained.

'Who is your prospective wife?' the woman demanded.

'Esi,' Asamoah replied.

'Wow!' Ha-ha-ha-a!' the woman yelled.

'Why?' Asamoah interrupted.

'Are you not making a mockery of yourself?' the woman snarled.

'Do you intend to insult me?' Asamoah said angrily.

'No,' the woman answered.

'Then why are those biting words?' Asamoah mumbled.

'Are you sure that Esi is your prospective wife?' the woman inquired.

'Yes. I can't lie to you?' Asamoah replied.

'How can a woman who has a husband be your prospective wife? Can two men marry one woman?' the woman asserted.

'What you are saying puzzles me? Do you mean that Esi has a husband?' Asamoah asked.

'Yes,' the woman answered.

'Wha-a-a-t! Do you really know Esi whom I'm talking about?' Asamoah asked.

'Is it not the one who sold this house to me?' the woman retorted.

'No. How can Esi, my prospective wife, sell this house to you without my knowledge?' Asamoah retorted.

'If Esi whom you are looking for is not the one who sold this house to me, then you've been misdirected to come to this house,' the woman explained.

'I've not been misdirected to this house. I'm the one who built this house for Esi, so how can I be misdirected to come here,' Asamoah snarled.

'Are you implying that you are the initial landlord of this house?' the woman inquired.

'Yes,' Asamoah replied.

'Then what happened?' asked the woman.

'I gave it to Esi to live in it,' Asamoah explained.

'Are you sure of what you are saying? Didn't you sell it to her?' the woman inquired.

'No. I gave it to her for free,' explained Asamoah.

'For free?' the woman asked with surprise.

'Yes,' Asamoah affirmed.

'For what reason?' the woman inquired.

'For being my prospective wife who had no good place to stay,' Asamoah explained.

'Are you not aware that Esi has gotten married?' the woman remarked.

'When?' asked Asamoah.

'In the last two weeks. Where were you then?' the woman asked.

'I was at Apram to do some important assignment for three weeks,' answered Asamoah.

'Esi has gotten married within those days,' the woman said.

'To whom?' Asamoah asked.

'I don't know the name of the husband,' the woman retorted.

'Where did their wedding take place?' Asamoah inquired.

'I don't know; she didn't tell me,' said the woman.

'Are you not lying?' asked Asamoah

'No,' the woman replied.

'How did you get to know that Esi has recently gotten married,' Asamoah asked.

'Before her wedding, she came to sell this house to me because she said she needed money to organize the wedding and after the wedding, she told me how successful it was,' the woman explained.

'Are you saying that Esi sold this house to you and used some of the proceeds to marry another man?' Asamoah inquired.

'Exactly!' the woman exclaimed.

'This is incredible,' Asamoah remarked and started sweating.

'Have you not been calling her on the phone to know her whereabouts?' the woman asked.

'For the past two weeks, anytime I called her, her phone was switched off. That is why I'm here to check on her,' Asamoah explained.

'Esi is not in the country,' the woman said.

'How come? Where is she?' Asamoah inquired.

'She has travelled with the husband to Britain,' the woman answered.

Asamoah, who was in astonishment, began to tremble uncontrollably and his countenance fell.

'How can Esi do this to me? I don't believe it. She can't dupe me like that. I will not allow her to dupe me,' Asamoah lamented.

'Don't you still believe me? Esi whom you claim is your prospective wife has married another man and has travelled with him to Britain. That is why she sold this house to me. I have the documents of the land,' the woman explained.

Wha-a-a-t? You are trespassing. Esi can't sell this house to you because she is not the rightful owner,' Asamoah argued.

After bouts of misunderstandings and arguments between Asamoah and the woman as to who was the rightful owner of the house, Asamoah went home dejected. Without delay, he went to Esi's mother in Abenso to ask of her, but the mother was not there.

Attempts to trace her proved futile. Investigations revealed that the woman whom Esi introduced Asamoah to, was not her mother and that they were not from Abenso. Esi conspired with her to dupe Asamoah.

When events had proved that Esi was not from Abenso, Asamoah made every effort to find her hometown and her parents, but it was in vain. Consequently, people reprimanded Asamoah for his inability to make credible background investigations about Esi, his fiancée, and condemned his decision to give his house to her in the name of love.

'How should Asamoah give his house to his fiancée? It is stupidity to do that,' a woman said.

'It is irrational to give a house that you have built for your parents to your fiancée. What if she does not marry you as it has happened to Asamoah?' a man remarked.

'One must be careful to let not love stupefy him to his own detriment like what has happened to Asamoah who has given his house to his fiancée only to be duped by her,' a boy said.

Asamoah, who had been duped by Esi, decided to take control of the house which Esi had sold to the woman, Akos, before her departure to Britain.

'I can still claim ownership of my house because everybody in this neighbourhood knows that the house is mine,' Asamoah thought.

Asamoah used different means, including threats to claim ownership of the house, but they were in vain. Akos who had bought the house from Esi took Asamoah to court and he was arraigned before the court. Since Akos was able to furnish the court with the documents of the house to prove her ownership, the court ruled that she was the legal owner of the house. Asamoah's thought of losing the ownership of the house and the harm Esi had caused him made him sick; he experienced sleeplessness and grew lean and pale.

'Why would Esi deceive me in the name of love? Why did I give my house to a woman whom I've not married yet? I don't understand this. Did Esi cast spells on me to love her in order to dupe me?' Asamoah thought.

CHAPTER TEN

Two months after the court case, Asamoah lost his job in a sugar factory; he was laid off following a reduction in the factory's sales. Before he was laid off, the manager of the factory had a discussion with him.

'Mr. Asamoah, it has become necessary that the factory must lay off some of the workers following the drastic reduction in its sales. In connection with this, the factory has decided to lay you off for the meantime, but promises to reinstate you when the situation warrants it,' the manager explained.

'Please, you should do something about it and retain me in the factory till the situation at hand is remedied,' Asamoah pleaded.

'As you are aware, the factory's sales are dwindling at an alarming rate, so it doesn't have enough money to pay salaries to many workers. You can't work for the factory while it cannot pay you. The factory's image will be in disrepute if it is unable to pay its workers. Therefore, we've decided to employ the number of workers the factory can afford to pay,' the manager explained.

Asamoah, who did not have anything to say again, had to accept the manager's decision to lay him off.

'Though I've lost my job, I'll not lose hope. Things will change for the better,' he thought and looked forward to the future with hope. However, he alternated between hope and despair when he began to experience financial and economic hardships. Asamoah had gone for a loan from a bank which he used to build the house he gave to Esi, but the loan was owing and when it was evident to that bank that he could not pay the loan following being laid off, the bank confiscated his remaining house that he had used as collateral in acquiring the loan. Consequently, he had no house to stay in, so he moved from friend to friend to beg them to accommodate him in their houses; he stayed in friend's houses in turns. Whenever he caught sight of the house he gave to Esi, he felt cheated and grieved over it.

'Some women are treacherous and cunning and Esi is no exception. If I had not given this house to Esi for the purpose of marrying her, I could have used some of the rooms for renting and my situation now wouldn't have been like this. Now, I have to beg friends to stay in their houses. Is this good?' Asamoah thought.

While people blamed him and heaped insults on him for being the cause of his plight; he decided to leave Pimso to avoid embarrassments. One night, he packed his belongings into a bag and travelled to Asim to look for a job.

'It is better for me to leave Pimso where I'm swallowed up in embarrassments and financial problems. There are also job opportunities in Asim and I can avail myself of one,' Asamoah pondered.

In Asim, Asamoah went from firm to firm and company to company to look for a job for a year until he got one in a textile company.

One evening, when it was 3 o'clock, Ama, having dressed decently, took her Bible and went from individual to individual to preach the word of God. She approached a young man, Baah and preached to him.

'Peace be unto you,' Ama greeted.

'Amen! The same unto you,' Baah responded.

'It interests me to discuss the word of God with you today,' Ama requested.

'No problem. You can do so,' said Baah.

'Thank you. I'm an evangelist and I attend Gateway Church. May I also know the church that you attend?' Ama remarked.

'Erm, erm, I used to attend church, but now I don't attend church,' Baah stammered.

'What church were you attending?' Ama inquired.

'Evergreen Church,' replied Baah.

'Why did you stop going?' asked Ama.

'Nothing,' Baah replied.

'Nothing? I don't understand it. There is a reason for you to stop going to the church,' Ama asserted.

'There is no reason,' Baah replied.

'Where you baptized in the church before you stopped going to church?' Ama inquired.

'No,' answered Baah.

'Are you sure that you were attending Evergreen Church?' Ama asked.

'Yes. I attended it for a short period,' Baah explained.

'For how long have you stopped going to the church?' Ama inquired.

'About fifteen years,' Baah answered.

'Then you were twenty years old,' Ama said with surprise.

'I was nineteen,' Baah retorted.

'This means that you are now thirty-four,' Ama asserted.

'Yes,' Baah said.

'Thank you for your cooperation and good answers. It is better late than never. I want to read something from the Bible to you. Can I do it?' Ama requested.

'Yes,' Baah retorted.

Ama unzipped her bag and took a Bible from it and gave it to Baah.

'This Bible is for you and after our discussion, I entreat you to read it daily,' Ama remarked.

'Thank you,' Baah said when he accepted it.

'Open the Bible to Matthew 16:26,' Ama instructed.

Baah flipped the leaflets of his Bible until he got to Matthew 16:26. While Ama read the words of the quotation, Baah used his forefinger to point at the words of the quotation in his Bible.

'Matthew 16:26; *what good will it be for a man if he gains the whole world, yet forfeits his soul? Or what can a man give in exchange for his soul?* This scripture shows that to be saved is infinitely better than to have everything in the world, but die unsaved,' Ama explained.

'What does it mean to die saved or unsaved?' asked Baah.

'When one dies and goes to heaven where there is eternal bliss, it means the person has died saved, but when one dies and goes to hell where there are endless sufferings and torments, it means the person has died unsaved,' explained Ama.

'How can one be saved?' Baah asked.

'Christian salvation is given by God through Jesus Christ. This means that Jesus Christ is the only means by whom one is saved. Romans 10:9; *that if you confess with your mouth, "Jesus is Lord," and believe in your heart that God raised him from the dead, you will be saved,*' Ama explained.

'After one has taken Jesus Christ as his Lord and personal saviour, can he be in the house without attending church, but do righteous things and go to heaven?' Baah inquired.

'It is an obligation for all people who take and confess Jesus Christ as their Lord and personal saviour to go to church where they will grow in the grace and knowledge of our Lord and Saviour Jesus Christ. Hebrews 10:25 says that *let us not give up meeting together, as some are in the habit of doing, but let us encourage one another...*' Ama explained.

'If it is so, then I have to seek a church where I will worship,' Baah retorted.

'Yes. You must do it with all alacrity. May God help you do it,' Ama remarked.

'So be it,' Baah said.

'This coming Sunday, I'll come and find out whether you will go to church,' Ama said.

'Then come and take me to church. I'll like to go to church with you,' Baah suggested.

'Really?' Ama exclaimed.

'Yes, I mean it. I've been postponing going to church for the past fifteen years,' Baah asserted.

'Then Sunday, I will come,' Ama assured him.

'At what time?' Baah inquired.

'7:30am,' Ama replied.

'Okay, I'll be expecting you,' said Baah.

'I'll like to bring the Bible discussion to an end,' Ama suggested.

'No problem. You can do so. Today, you have given me insight into the word of God and have purged my mind of certain misconceptions and heresies. Thank you,' Baah asserted.

'Should you say the closing prayer?' Ama requested.

'No. You must say it,' Baah replied sharply.

'Then let's close our eyes,' Ama instructed and prayed.

'Oh God! We thank you that you have let us have a successful Bible discussion, Amen.'

'Amen!' Baah responded.

Ama shook hands with Baah to congratulate him on his active participation in the Bible discussion.

'You've done very well for the contributions you made in the Bible discussion. You can be a good Bible teacher,' Ama remarked.

'Amen!' Baah shouted.

When Ama was walking on the roadside to the house, a car which came across her stopped and the driver called out to her.

'Ama, come. Let me take you to where you are going?'

When Ama reached the car, it was Akoto, her rejected suitor who was the driver.

'Let me take you to where you are going,' Akoto reiterated.

'Thank you. I want to exercise my body by walking to the house,' Ama explained.

'From here to your house is quite long. Let me take you there,' Akoto insisted.

'Thank you. It is okay. I want to exercise my body by walking to the house,' Ama reiterated.

'Refusing to accept my offer to take you to your house shows that you have a grudge against me,' Akoto muttered.

'No. I don't have any grudge against you. What wrong have you done to me that I should have a grudge against you?' Ama explained.

'It is said actions speak louder than words,' Akoto asserted.

'Do my actions show hostility towards you?' Ama inquired.

'Of course,' replied Akoto.

'What actions?' Ama inquired.

'Your action of refusing to board my car,' Akoto explained.

'Okay let's go,' Ama said and went into the car and Akoto drove her to the house.

'Thank you,' Ama said when she alighted from the car.

'Thanks belong to God,' Akoto retorted.

Being hungry, Ama went to the kitchen to prepare her supper; she collected tomatoes, pepper, onions and other food ingredients into a silver dish and washed them. When she had chopped them into preferable pieces, she boiled them to prepare a delicious stew. While the stew was simmering, Ama used a ladle to stir it intermittently until it was well cooked and edible. She then peeled cocoyam, sliced them and boiled them and ate it with the stew.

When Ama had taken the supper and was relaxing on a sofa, the mother went to her.

'Have a seat and let me give you something to eat,' Ama said.

'Don't bother yourself. I'm full,' the mother retorted.

'How are you and dad?' Ama inquired.

'We are fine. Where have you been? About three hours ago, I came here, but you weren't around,' the mother said.

'I went for evangelism,' Ama explained.

'That is very good, but it is also good to have a partner who will help you in evangelism. Thus, I'm here to hear good news from you,' the mother asserted.

'What partner do I need?' Ama interrupted sharply.

'A marriage partner. I want you to marry so you can bear me grandchildren,' the mother explained.

'What good news do you want to hear from me?' Ama inquired.

'Your decision to marry Akoto, that noble and well-to-do young man,' the mother replied.

'I'll not marry him,' Ama said quickly and stood up to go to the room, but the mother grabbed her by the right hand.

'Why are you going away while my discussion with you is inconclusive?' the mother muttered.

'How many times do you want me to tell you that I'll not marry Akoto?' Ama said when she had sat down.

'Every caring mother wants her daughter to have good things in life, including having a good husband. That is why I want you to marry Akoto who will be a good husband to you. You must not forget the saying that you can tell a ripe corn by its look,' the mother explained.

'Akoto can't be a good husband to me and therefore, I'll not marry him,' said Ama.

'You are a child, so you must listen to your parents. Our elders say the eye brows grow before the bead. Your parents are more experienced and knowledgeable than you,' the mother explained.

'Mum, don't you believe that God will give me a husband who is better than Akoto?' Ama asked.

'In terms of what?' the mother demanded.

'In terms of everything,' answered Ama.

'Is everything includes money?' the mother inquired.

'Yes,' replied Ama.

'In terms of money, Akoto is okay for you. It has been said a bird in the hand is worth two in the bush. Nowadays, it is not easy to have a well-to-do young man, who is God-fearing like Akoto as a husband,' the mother retorted.

CHAPTER ELEVEN

When Ama had seen the mother off after the conversation, she went to the room to watch a movie which was about the coming of Jesus Christ. The movie which was didactic and thrilling made her decide to show it to the public as part of her evangelism.

'This movie is good and it is based on the word of God. When unbelievers watch it, it can make them repent and become Christians. Therefore, I'll find time and means of showing it to the public,' Ama thought.

When the movie came to an end, it was 9:20pm and she went to bed after she had prayed.

'Oh God! I thank you for the day's activities. I beseech you to protect me from the attacks of demons while I sleep. Oh God! May you let a man who is God-fearing and of noble character and can take good care of me come and marry me, Amen.'

As Ama lay on her bed pondering on the words of her mother in their last meeting, she fell asleep and had a dream in which she was wearing a wedding gown and was holding the right hand of a cripple called Arko in her church and they were standing before a pastor who laid his hands on them to bless their wedding.

'What God has put together, let not man put asunder. Therefore, I put Arko and you together as a husband and a wife in the name of Jesus, Amen!' the pastor said.

The moment the pastor said, 'Amen' in the dream, Ama woke up suddenly and realized that she was dreaming.

'Why marrying a cripple? No. Isaiah 55:8; *for my thoughts are not your thoughts, neither are your ways my ways, declares the LORD.*James 1:17; *every good and prefect gift is from above, coming down from the Father of the heavenly lights, who does not change like shifting shadows,*' Ama reflected on these scriptures and knelt down and put her Bible before her and raised her hands to pray.

'Oh God! Let this dream come to pass according to your will, but not according to my will, Amen.'

In the morning when Ama had taken her breakfast, she went to look for Arko, the cripple who was in a wheelchair and was singing Christian songs. Arko was a good and talented singer who had been earning a living from singing after completing senior high school. He was fair in complexion and had an oval chin and symmetrical teeth which matched his symmetrical lips. His natural curly hair accentuated his good looks and most people described him as the most handsome man in the church, a quality which had endeared him to most people.

'Praise the Lord!' Ama shouted.

'Amen!' Arko responded.

'It is a pleasure for me to visit you today,' Ama said.

'Thank you,' Arko retorted.

'Last Sunday, I didn't see you at church. Why?' Ama asked.

'I wasn't well; Malaria attacked me,' Arko explained.

'Oh sorry! Are you now well?' Ama ascertained.

'Yes,' replied Akoto.

'Then may the name of God be praised,' Ama said.

'Amen!' Arko shouted.

'Have you heard that Ofori and Efia are going to have their wedding next month?' Ama asked.

'Yes,' Arko answered.

'Will you attend it?' Ama inquired.

'I've not decided yet,' Arko retorted.

'You must try to attend it, so that you can have more information to help you organize yours,' Ama suggested.

'Me? Having a wedding?' Arko exclaimed.

'Yes. Won't you marry?' Ama retorted.

'Now, I've not thought of marrying,' Arko explained.

'Then you must think of it,' Ama suggested.

'Really?' Arko exclaimed.

'Yes. You can be a good husband,' Ama retorted.

'To whom?' Arko inquired.

'To any woman,' Ama replied.

'Any woman like who?' Arko demanded.

'Like me,' answered Ama.

'Like you?' Arko asked.

'Yes,' Ama affirmed.

'May it come to pass,' Arko said hilariously.

'Amen!' Ama yelled.

Ama presented a beautiful rose to Arko and asked permission to go home. When Sunday arrived, Ama went to take Baah to church.

'Peace be unto you,' Ama greeted.

'Amen!' Baah responded.

'I've come for us to go to church together,' said Ama.

'You've done very well. Thank you. I thought you would not come. I've even forgotten that I told you to come and take me to church today, so I've not prepared for church. However, may you exercise patience and wait for me to go and bath,' Baah asserted.

'No problem. I'm waiting for you,' Ama retorted.

Baah rushed to the bathroom and took his bath. When Baah was ready, he went to Ama who was sitting in an armchair and was reading her Bible.

'Let's go. I'm ready,' Baah said.

'Where is your Bible?' asked Ama.

'I don't have one,' answered Baah.

'During our last meeting, I gave you a Bible,' Ama said.

'Yes. You did, but I've given it to my younger brother. Let me go for it,' Baah said and hurried to collect the Bible from the younger brother who was in his room.

'You are not reading the Bible,' Ama complained.

'From today, I will start reading it,' Baah said assuredly.When Ama and Baah were going to church, they met Baah's friend on the way who talked with Baah.

'I'm coming to your house. Where are you going?' the friend asked.

'I'm going to church,' answered Baah.

'You are lying? Do you go to church? Have you been to church before? See your friend off and let us go and drink. I have bottles of beer there,' Baah's friend asserted.

'To drink?' Ama interrupted.

'Yes,' replied Baah's friend.

'Drunkenness is not good; it is destructive,' Ama explained.

'I'll not drink again,' Baah asserted.

'Can you stop drinking? You are lying,' Baah's friend retorted.

'I mean it,' said Baah.

'Are you trying to say that you are also born-again?' Baah's friend asked.

'Precisely,' replied Baah.

'Born-again has become a common term that most people use to describe themselves while in reality they are not. They use it to conceal their bad deeds. Do you want to be like those hypocritical people?' Baah's friend explained.

'God will help me not to be like those people,' Baah replied.

Fifteen minutes after Ama and Baah had gone to the church; the pastor of the church preached the sermon which hinged on Christian salvation.

'Repent for the kingdom of God is at hand. What good will it be for a man if he gains the whole world, yet forfeits his soul?'

When the pastor had finished preaching, he called those who were not members of the church, but wanted to worship with them.

'At this juncture, I'll like to call the strangers among us who want to worship with us to come forward?'

Baah who was moved by the pastor's preaching and was prepared to worship with the church stood up and walked majestically to where the pastor was standing.

'Are you prepared to accept Jesus Christ as your Lord and personal saviour?' the pastor asked.

'Yes,' answered Baah.

'Then you must say these words after me,' the pastor instructed.

'I, Baah, accept Jesus Christ who died on the cross for my sins and was raised for my justification as my Lord and personal saviour...Amen!' Baah affirmed.

From that day, Baah always went to church and practiced the word of God in keeping with his confession; he led a Christian life worth of commendation.

With the passage of time, Ama often visited Arko and gave him gifts. At times, she went to take him to church by pushing his wheelchair. One day, when Arko was in his wheelchair while Ama was pushing it, Arko's mother who met them at the entrance of the house remarked, 'Ama, I'll give Arko to you in marriage.'

'Ha-ha-ha-a! You must do it without delay,' Ama retorted.

'Then I'll inform your parents about it,' Arko's mother remarked.

'That is the right thing to do,' said Ama.

When they entered the house, Ama commented on Arko's mother's statement.

'Did you hear what your mother said at the entrance?' asked Ama.

'Yes,' replied Arko,

'What did she say?' Ama demanded.

'She said that she would give me to you in marriage,' Arko recounted.

'Exactly,' Ama yelled, 'but why don't you act on your mother's statement?'

'Can I be your husband?' asked Arko.

'Yes. You can be my husband hundred percent,' Ama answered.

'Are you joking?' Arko asked with doubt.

'No. I'm very serious,' Ama retorted.

Arko, who still didn't believe that Ama was willing to marry him, continued to ask her questions.

'Can you love me?' asked Arko.

'Yes. I love you already, but not I can love you,' Ama explained.

'What shows that you love me already?' Arko demanded.

'It said actions speak louder than words,' Ama retorted.

'So can I inform my parents about my decision to marry you?' Arko asked.

'Yes. You must do it with the assurance that I'm prepared to be your wife,' Ama said.

'Then I'll pray about it to seek the approval of God,' Arko asserted.

'That is the best thing to do,' Ama said happily.

While Arko and Ama were courting, some of the townspeople gossiped about them. Some of them castigated Ama for courting Arko, saying that she had made a wrong choice.

'Why should Ama reject all the rich men who wanted to marry her and choose to marry Arko who cannot work to take care of her? It may be that Arko has cast spells on her to love him,' two young men gossiped.

When Ama's parents got to know that Ama and Arko were courting, they didn't believe it, so they summoned her to ascertain the truth.

'Ama, you have reached a marriageable age and I want you to have a responsible husband, but you've turned a deaf ear to my suggestions,' the father said.

'God has answered my prayer,' Ama interrupted.

'What prayer?' the father demanded.

'My prayer to get a suitable husband?' answered Ama.

'Have you got a suitable man who wants to marry you?' the father asked.

'Yes,' answered Ama.

'Where is he from?' the father demanded.

'He is from this town,' Ama replied.

'This town?' the father shouted in astonishment.

'Yes,' Ama affirmed.

'Who is he?' the father demanded.

80

'Arko,' Ama answered.

'Do I know him?' the father asked.

'Yes,' Ama replied.

'Who is he?' the father asked.

'Auntie Aku's son,' Ama explained.

'That cripple?' the father inquired.

'Yes. To be physically challenged is not a disability. A disabled person is someone who is not in Christ,' Ama retorted.

'What has come into your mind? Are you joking?' the father mumbled.

'I'm not joking. Arko is the man whom I love,' Ama explained.

'Shut up! What do you know about love?' the father thundered.

'Ama, you have surprised me. Why do you go for Arko who is not in a good position to take care of you? What makes Arko better than Akoto whom I want you to marry?' the mother intervened.

'It is only God who knows,' Ama replied.

'It is my duty to make sure that you marry someone who can take good care of you. What money has Arko got to marry you? Are you charmed by his good looks?' the father interrupted.

'No. I'm influenced by the direction of God to marry him,' explained Ama.

'Are you trying to mean that it God who has directed you to marry Arko?' the father inquired.

'Exactly,' replied Ama.

'Don't let your being an evangelist deceive you? Why will God direct you to marry someone who cannot take good care of you, but creates financial problems for you?' the father remarked.

'The ways of God transcend the logic of men. God's ways and directions are perfect regardless of the forms they take,' Ama explained.

Ama's father and mother tried to dissuade her from marrying Arko, but to no avail. Many of her friends voiced their resentments over her decision to marry Arko, but she did not listen to them.

'Ama, why should you marry Arko who cannot take care of you? There are noble rich men in the church who are willing to marry you, so why should you decide to marry Arko, a pauper? You must not marry him,' Ama's friend said.

'Ama, for you to marry Arko will not augur well for your progress and prosperity because he can't provide your needs. This means you are the only person who will provide for the family. Will this help you?' another friend suggested.

'My decision to marry Arko has divine approval and anything of divine approval is excellent and will triumph. Therefore, I have no fear to marry him,' Ama explained.

As days elapsed, Arko told his parents and other relatives his decision to marry Ama and they did not hesitate to ask for Ama's hand in marriage from her relatives for him. Ama's parents who initially opposed the marriage had no choice than to accept Arko's proposal to marry Ama from his relatives. Accordingly, a day was earmarked for the wedding ceremony which became the topic for discussion among people.

'This is the first time in this neighbourhood that a man who is a cripple and a woman are going to have a wedding in the church,' a woman remarked.

'The church has become the platform for some people to have husbands and wives and Arko is one of those people. Arko has got a wife by his going to church. The church leaders have given Arko to Ama in marriage,' a twenty-nine-year-old man slandered.

During the wedding ceremony, many people including the church members, pastors, non-church members, media men and pagans who wanted to see how a cripple would conduct himself for the wedding ceremony attended it. During the wedding march, Ama walked beside Arko who was in a wheelchair pushed by a young adult. This spectacular event attracted the attention of all and sundry and was greeted with an extraordinary outpouring of applause and jubilations. Such an epoch-making event spread the canopy of fame over Arko and Ama in Pimso and its environs.

'We don't need any further evidence that Arko and Ama's wedding is not ordinary; it is by divine providence. I've attended many wedding ceremonies including that of celebrities, but none can be compared to this one in terms of splendour and organization,' an old man remarked.

When Arko and Ama took the marriage vows to remain inseparable until death, something miraculous happened which made the wedding ceremony unprecedented and historic in Pimso and its surrounding towns and villages. The moment Arko finished affirming the words of the marriage vow after the officiating pastor; he stood up from his wheelchair, shouting that he had been healed in the name of Jesus.

'My legs have received divine strength to walk the moment I said, 'Amen' to conclude the marriage vow. May the name of God be praised,' he testified while jumping and dancing to demonstrate his healing.

'O-o-o-oh! This is strange. It is too miraculous for Arko to be healed in this way. Arko's healing is beyond human understanding. Arko's marriage to Ama is a blessing because it has healed him of his sickness which has defied medical solution,' a girl testified.

'The logic of God transcends the logic of all people in all generations. God has used Ama's marriage to Arko as a direction to heal Arko of a condition that no human medicine can cure. This explains that Ama's marriage to Arko has God's approval. Therefore, it is better to rely on God for everything, including your marriage than to rely on your human wisdom and requirements,' a man asserted.

'No scientific laws and theories can explain Arko's healing. May the name of God be praised,' a boy said with great wonder.

There were jubilations, merrymaking, drumming, singing and dancing all over the place. News about Arko's healing circulated everywhere and it astounded the people who heard it. Many radio and television stations discussed it. Consequently, some people presented gifts to Ama for her unwavering decision to marry Arko in the face of castigations, insinuations and disapproval of some people.

Three months after the wedding ceremony, it was published in newspapers and reported on the radio and televisions that four armed robbers had been arrested by the police. Consequently, the pictures of the armed robbers were shown on the front pages of newspapers, and televisions. To the surprise of the people of Pimso, Akoto was one of the armed robbers.

'Is Akoto an armed robber? Eh! This world is full of mysteries. Did Akoto have his money through robbery?' a woman who knew him asserted.

When Ama's father and mother who insisted that Ama should marry Akoto heard that Akoto had been caught in an armed robbery and saw him on the front pages of newspapers, they were amazed and then believed that he was not a suitable marriage partner for Ama.

'We didn't have an iota of thought that Akoto could be a treacherous person let alone be an armed robber. He made us believe that he is a godly man by his behaviour and the use of Christian jargons. The saying that all that glitters is not gold has definite rings of truth to it,' Ama's parents remarked.

'If I had listened to you to marry Akoto, where would be my fate now? Is it not problems?' Ama asserted.

Akoto was arraigned before the court and when all is said and done, the court sentenced him to forty-five years imprisonment in hard labour.

'Ama, if you had married Akoto, could you divorce him for the reason that he had been sentenced to forty-five years imprisonment and marry again?' Ama's friend asked.

'No; it is not biblical to divorce your husband and marry again when he is jailed for forty-five years,' Ama answered.

'Then could you have waited faithfully for him without committing adultery during his forty-five years in prison?' the friend inquired.

'It needs divine strength. God knew all these things that is why he didn't allow me to marry him,' Ama retorted.

'Then it is good to rely on God for everything, including your marriage so that He will help you to achieve victory and excellence,' the friend remarked.

'Surely!' Ama exclaimed.

Arko and Ama enjoyed peace and stability in their marriage and had three children. Exactly two years after their marriage, Arko became a prophet of God who healed many people including the lame, the cripple, the blind and many others in the name of Jesus. He travelled to many countries to preach the word of God amid healing and the performing of miracles in name of Jesus to save the lives of people.

CHAPTER TWELVE

While Amoako was standing at the car station in confusion, Sarpong came.

'You are welcome,' Sarpong said.

'Thank you,' Amoako retorted dejectedly.

'Where is your luggage?' Sarpong inquired.

'A thief has snatched it from me,' Amoako answered.

'When?' Sarpong asked.

'When I was calling you on the phone,' Amoako explained.

'Is your money in it?' asked Sarpong.

'Yes,' Amoako replied.

'You have been careless. Let's go home,' Sarpong snarled.

On reaching home, Sarpong went to the market to buy items of clothing and a bag for Amoako after which they conversed.

'Our company has declared vacancies in the procurement unit, so I want you to apply for employment?' said Sarpong.

'Has the company advertised the vacancies in the newspapers?' Amoako inquired.

'Yes,' answered Sarpong.

'When?' Amoako asked.

'A week ago,' Sarpong replied.

'Are there vacancies in the department where you work?' Amoako asked.

'No,' answered Sarpong.

'What is the deadline for the submission of applications?' Amoako inquired.

'Next week,' Sarpong answered.

'Then I must hurry up to submit my application,' Amoako remarked.

'Yes. You must hurry up. The deadline is nearer that is why I've let you come here to submit your application,' said Sarpong.

On the following day, Amoako wrote an application letter, stating his credentials and submitted it to the personnel manager and eagerly looked forward to hearing positive reply from the company. Two weeks later, Amoako received a letter from the company that he had been shortlisted for an interview.

On the day of the interview, Amoako dressed gorgeously; he wore a dark suit of excellent embroidery, a pair of spectacles and a tie to match a pair of black shoes and went to the interview. Amoako, who was an academic prodigy, was able to answer correctly all the questions that the interviewers asked him. Accordingly, the interviewers, being impressed by his performance and comportment, selected him for the job as the procurement officer. Thus, the company served him with an appointment letter which outlined the conditions of service.

Amoako, upon receiving the appointment letter, bounced with joy and began to make guesses and mental calculations of how he was going to enjoy a good standard of living.

'I've suffered severe economic and financial hardships due to unemployment. Now that I've got a job, I'm going to eat sumptuous meals and drive in a posh car,' Amoako thought.

When Amoako started work as the procurement officer in the company and earned salary, his financial situation improved considerably, so he built a house and bought two cars for personal use. Now that Amoako has achieved economic independence as well as financial stability, he decided to have a wife, but he was not getting a woman who met his beauty requirement to marry.

'My wife must be exquisite; she must be an epitome of real, but uncommon beauty,' Amoako always told his friends.

When Amoako had worked for six years and had passed the age of thirty, but had still not married, some of the people in his vicinity including some of his friends began to cast insinuations and castigations at him.

'For a prominent and well-to-do man like Amoako to be a bachelor could mean that he is impotent,' a young woman remarked.

'What prevents Amoako from marrying? Is it money? No. Is it unemployment? No. Are there no women in the country? No. Then it is only impotence that will make a man of prominent position like Amoako to remain unmarried,' two men insinuated.

At Amoako's workplace, some of the workers also teased him to marry.

'This meeting is not meant for bachelors. It is not meant for people who have no responsibilities to perform in their homes. It is meant for those who can think and reason as husbands. Who are you? When those of us who have wives and children are talking, you are also talking,' his co-worker ridiculed him in a heated argument on financial matters during a business meeting. They nearly fought had it not been the intervention of the director of the company.

That day, Amoako went home dejected and decided to look for a wife. He combed every nook and cranny of Pimso for a wife and kept an eye on almost all the women in his vicinity in order to choose the one who met his requirements like a buyer who had gone to the market and was comparing the quality of commodities from store to store.

Upon a thorough search, Amoako finally found a woman who met his beauty requirement. The woman was called Ansaba and was a native of Pimso, but she stayed in Accra. She only went to Pimso on occasions like funerals, wedding ceremonies, festivals and Christmas.

Amoako met her at a wedding ceremony he had attended. At the wedding, Ansaba went to sit beside Amoako and when he set eyes on her, he was mesmerized by her beauty and interacted with her by asking her name in a clever way.

'Are you Benewaah who was sent by Dr. Abu some time ago to come for some financial documents from me?' Amoako asked.

'No; I'm not the one,' Ansaba replied.

'Then you resemble Benewaah whom I'm talking about. Anyway, I'm Amoako,' Amoako said in a jovial way.

I'm Ansaba.'

'Very good. You are welcome,' Amoako remarked hysterically.

'Thank you,' Ansaba retorted.

When the bridegroom and the bride appeared on the scene, they stopped conversing and watched the proceedings of the wedding ceremony, but when the wedding ceremony was over, Amoako chatted at length with her.

'I stay at the back of the Police Station. If you pass that area, try to visit me. Where do you also stay?' Amoako asked.

'I stay in the house painted yellow adjacent to the Post Office,' Ansaba answered.

'I've seen that house. One of my co-workers who had gone on transfer used to stay there. If I pass that area, I'll come to the house to inquire of you,' Amoako asserted.

'That will be good of you, but don't come on a market day. On market days, I help my aunt to sell in her store,' Ansaba explained.

'I'll not allow my visit to interfere with the performance of your household chores as well as your commercial duties at the market. When are you leaving for Accra?' Amoako inquired.

'I can't tell you the exact time that I'll leave for Accra, but I hope to spend two months here,' replied Ansaba.

After the conversation, they exchanged phone numbers, said goodbye to each other and parted company. When Amoako went home, he had unusual feelings for Ansaba because he had fallen in love with her.

'I can't afford to lose this woman of extraordinary beauty. I've found my wife,' Amoako soliloquized.

Indeed, Ansaba was an epitome of real beauty; she was slim, chocolate in complexion and had a radiant face and pointed nose. When she smiled the expression of her face was enough to make a man admire her. In terms of beauty, she was an apple of every man's eye. For this reason, at the age of twenty-eight, she had received about a thousand messages of love from many different men, ranging from celebrities to people of low social class.

One afternoon, when Amoako visited her in the house, she received him with happiness. Before Ansaba asked him his mission, he had already started saying it.

'Since I've the welfare of humanity at heart, I've come to visit you to ask of your welfare and find out how you are coping with the circumstances of life because most people are complaining that life is difficult and unbearable nowadays.'

'I'm alive and kicking and everything is fine. Thank you,' Ansaba retorted.

'Ansaba, I deem it necessary to thank you for your good reception. This shows how you uphold the value of hospitality in our tradition. I'll like to leave, but I'll be most grateful if you could come to my house this Saturday, so that we will go for a lunch,' Amoako remarked.

'Okay, if I have nothing doing by then, I'll come,' Ansaba asserted and saw Amoako off.

On the following day, when Amoako's friends went to him in the house, he told them about Ansaba.

'It interests me to tell you that I've seen a woman who surpasses all the women in this vicinity in terms of beauty. She is really my choice. Everything about her is perfect,' Amoako boasted.

'Does she have big buttocks?' a friend asked humorously.

'She has rounded and medium-sized buttocks,' Amoako replied.

'Who is she?' another friend asked.

'She is called Ansaba and lives in Accra, but she came here for a wedding ceremony. She has told me that she would spend two months here before she would go back to Accra. I'll make sure I woo her before she goes back to Accra,' Amoako said.

'Good! Congrats!' another friend yelled.

'You must take your time to study her. Some women are treacherous; they cause serious problems to their husbands. All that glitters is not gold,' another friend asserted.

'There is nothing to be afraid of. I can handle her if it happens that she proves stubborn, but I'm sure that she will be of good character. You can tell a ripe corn by its look,' Amoako retorted.

Amoako and his friends shook hands in turns while they called out their nicknames and parted company.

To fulfill her promise, Ansaba also visited Amoako in the house.

'You must have a seat to make yourself comfortable because you have come to the house of a true friend,' Amoako said.

'Thank you,' said Ansaba.

'You've given me surprise because I thought you would not come to visit me. You are therefore wholeheartedly welcome,' Amoako asserted.

'Thank you,' Ansaba retorted.

After their conversation, Amoako took Ansaba to a restaurant for a lunch where they enjoyed themselves with sumptuous meal and soft drinks. Again, Amoako took her to different stores for shopping and bought her expensive items which included a wrist watch, a mobile phone, necklaces, pairs of sandals and dresses as an expression of generosity.

CHAPTER THIRTEEN

A month later, Amoako called Ansaba on the phone and asked her to meet him under a mango tree at exactly 10:00am. Ansaba who was eager to know what Amoako had for her did not hesitate to meet him under the mango tree.

'Even though marriage is a matter of choice, it will be an indelible blemish in one's life if one does not marry throughout his or her life on earth.

'If some years ago we were kids and immature to talk about marriage, I think the time is ripe for us to do so. Ansaba, my few days encounter with you is clear evidence that we can be good marriage partners. I'm very interested in you, so I want to marry you. It is not the time for me to take you as a girlfriend, bearing in mind that we have bypassed a boy-girl relationship,' Amoako said.

Upon deep reflection and metal calculations of the advantages and disadvantages of being married at her age, Ansaba accepted Amoako's proposal. Having dated each other for three months, they married.

'My newly-married couple, marriage like any other events has a lot of problems. Whether you like it or not, problems will come, but when problems come, the two of you must come together to solve them. You must continue to exhibit the kind of love, respect and character which have brought you together as a husband and a wife. Temptations are ahead of you, so you must be prepared to endure them. You are now one, so live as one and do everything with unity of minds,' the officiating pastor advised Amoako and Ansaba.

As a newly-married couple, Amoako and Ansaba lived at peace with each other. However, when they had lived for a year, the kind of love, care, behaviour and attitude they had exhibited towards each other changed. Ansaba started to behave badly; she occasionally quarreled with Amoako and stopped sweeping the house, tidying up rooms and washing Amoako's clothes. She also stopped cooking for him, explaining that when she continued to cook for him and do other household chores, the beauty of her body would be marred. She therefore asked him to employ a maid to do all the household chores.

Amoako, who was easily provoked, did not take her suggestion kindly.

'Nonsense! You can't dictate to me. No way! I'm not going to pamper you. Never!' Amoako roared at her while stamping his foot on the ground to emphasize seriousness.

What is more? As a married woman, Ansaba would go on outings with her friends without the consent of Amoako. At times, she would go home very late in the night and give excuses to Amoako to justify herself. Such an attitude on her part generated disputes between them.

One day, when Amoako was sitting on a chair and was reading a story book, Ansaba went to sit beside him and gave him tantalizing and passionate kisses on his cheeks with all humility.

'My sweetheart, things are changing with the passage of time. We must also change some of our ways of doing things. In view of this, I think the car we are using is outmoded for top officials like you. Therefore, I suggest that you buy a new and fashionable car so that we will use that one for going to functions and meetings. Last week, my friend, Awo, and her husband changed their car for a new and fashionable one,' she explained.

The moment Ansaba finished saying this; Amoako shouted at her.

'Stupid! What do you take me for? Since you have got someone to provide you with three square meals a day and provide for your upkeep without working for it, you don't think. It is stupid to tell me that.'

'If I'm stupid, then you are what? Birds of a feather flock together,' Ansaba snapped.

'Is that what you are telling me? We live to see,' Amoako snarled.

In the evening, when they went to bed, Ansaba intentionally put on a pair of skin-tight jeans and spread a bed sheet on the floor and slept on it while Amoako slept on the bed. Amoako, who did not understand her new attitude, tried to figure out why she was sleeping on the floor in a pair of skin-tight jeans.

'Ansaba, why are you sleeping on the floor instead of joining me in bed? It is 9:00pm and you know what to do as a wife,' Amoako muttered as he woke her up.

'You must not disturb me. How can I sleep on the same bed with a man who has no regard for his wife's suggestions and requests? Will you buy the car? If no, you must allow me to sleep on the floor,' Ansaba said.

Amoako lost his temper by her statement and grabbed her and pulled her to the bed while she resisted him.

'What do you want to imply?' Amoako roared.

'I'm implying that you should buy the car,' replied Ansaba.

That night, they ran a hundred metres in the room; Amoako had to run after Ansaba like a hunter who was chasing a rat to catch to send her to bed in order to make love with her.

Indeed, the idea of Ansaba refusing to make love with Amoako, her husband, as a means to claim her demands was inappropriate and morally wrong. Such an attitude weakens the foundation of a stable marriage. Thus, it erodes love, the very ingredient, which gives flavour and stability to marriage.

Moreover, Ansaba spent money extravagantly; she would buy expensive things such as dresses on credit for Amoako to pay without his initial consent. She also prevented Amoako's sisters from going to visit him in the house and quarreled with them on many occasions.

Amoako did everything he could to make her change her attitude but no avail; he reported her to her parents and other noble people to advise her to change her attitude, but she was adamant. When Amoako and Ansaba had lived for one and half years, Ansaba conceived and gave birth to fraternal twins, a boy and a girl and they named them Ampah and Asabea respectively. However, when Ampah and Asabea were four years old, Amoako divorced Ansaba because of her behaviour which he could no longer tolerate.

One morning, Ansaba rushed to Amoako's office at the workplace and quarreled with him. When the managing director of the company made an attempt to sack her from the office because her presence there at that time was against the company's rules, she insulted him in the hearing of everyone who was at the office. She also tore into pieces official documents that Amoako was signing for the managing director to be sent to South Africa on that day.

Consequently, Amoako was held responsible and had to pay for his wife's impudent behaviour and gross misconduct; he was sacked from the company. According to an official statement explaining his dismissal, he was sacked because the destruction of the official documents by his wife caused a huge financial loss to the company. When Amoako was sacked, he divorced Ansaba.

When Ansaba was asked why she rushed to Amoako's office to behave badly, she explained that Amoako had been telling people that she was not a respectful wife, so she went there to prove her disrespectfulness to him.

'Is that how you are? You didn't behave well at all. Now, have you seen the harm you have caused to your husband and yourself? Who will take care of your children now that your husband has lost his job? Barima, Ansaba's uncle said.

Many other people, including some of her friends, rebuked her for her uncouth behaviour.

'Ansaba, why did you do that? You have not only brought shame to yourself, but also a bad name to your family. If your husband was at fault, you could have used appropriate means to correct him instead of going to quarrel with him at his workplace,' her friend rebuked her.

When Amoako divorced Ansaba, he took the male twin, Ampah, to stay with him while Ansaba stayed with Asabea, the female twin.

Having lost his job and divorced his wife, Amoako moved to Accra to live there to look for a job. At Accra, he met his intimate friend who had then come back from the United States of America. The friend Obeng was his good friend from junior high school to university. At university, they were always together, but their friendship seemed to go into extinction when Obeng left for the United States of America soon after graduating from the university.

'It was a long time since we saw and heard from each other. In fact, you didn't try at all. No letter, no call,' Amoako blamed Obeng.

'The activities up there make one too busy that he hardly calls home,' Obeng retorted.

'What brought you to Ghana?' Amoako inquired.

'Having obtained a master's degree in Business Entrepreneurship, I've come to establish business ventures here to offer jobs to my compatriots who are unemployed,' answered Obeng.

'Oh nice! That is a very good idea. I used to work with a gold mining company, but I was dismissed from the company because of the behaviour of my wife whom I have divorced,' Amoako narrated his past experiences to Obeng.

'Oh! Sorry for such unfortunate experiences. They are a part of life,' Obeng consoled Amoako.

CHAPTER FOURTEEN

With time, Obeng made arrangements for Amoako to travel to the United States of America. He helped Amoako to acquire the necessary traveling documents and assisted him financially. When Amoako was going to the United States of America, he gave his twin son, Ampah, to Obeng and his wife, Fosuah, to take care of since they were not having a child at that time. Obeng and his wife took good care of Ampah, providing all his basic needs. All along, Ampah did not know of his biological mother, Ansaba and his twin sister.

At the age of six, Ampah started basic school. As seconds accumulated into minutes, minutes into hours, hours into days, days into months, and months into years, Ampah completed junior high school and went to senior high school. When he was in the final year of senior high school, he was made the senior school prefect because of his unequalled academic performance, good leadership skills as well as his comportment. However, two months after Ampah had been made the senior prefect, his friend Bimpong, who was the leader of his campaign team during the election of the school prefects, asked him to behave a girlfriend.

'Ampah, now that you are a senior prefect of the school, you need to be active in all areas including relationship. You must have a girlfriend. I can link you to any girl of your choice. After all, the girls in the school are under your authority, so it is very easy to have one as a girlfriend,' Bimpong suggested.

'Don't pester me with love issues. As the senior school prefect, I'm one of the custodians of the school rules and regulations, so I must lead an exemplary life for others to emulate. I won't take a girlfriend in the school,' Ampah retorted.

'Don't be an ancient boy but you must be abreast of time. The senior prefects in the senior high schools in the country have girlfriends. Are you trying to tell me that they are not ensuring discipline in their schools? Don't be too ancient. If those of us who are at the grassroots have girlfriends, how much more a whole senior prefect? You will be a laughing stock if senior prefects in other schools get to know that you a senior prefect who has no girlfriend,' Bimpong said.

When Ampah pondered over what Bimpong had told him, he did not accept his suggestion to take a girlfriend. However, upon persistent ridicule and pressure from Bimpong and other friends, he finally made up his mind to take a girlfriend as a senior prefect whether or not it was good.

One afternoon, he approached a girl, Asabea, and proposed to her. Asabea was very brilliant and eloquent and was nicknamed The English Parrot because of how she spoke English with a considerable command and fluency. When it comes to beauty she was exceptional. During a beauty contest organized in the school as part of the entertainment programme, she was adjudged the most beautiful girl in the school by all and sundry.

'Asabea, from the first year to the final year, I see you to be unique and outstanding among the girls in terms of behaviour and comportment. Such girls of your calibre need corresponding and befitting partners to pair with if relationship or marriage becomes necessary.

'Asabea, I find you lovable. You are not meant for the riff-raff; you are meant for high class and noble people who have noble character like me. I'm interested in you. School is a place where people from different backgrounds meet to interact with one another in order to make friends, including choosing future marriage partners to suit their individual idiosyncrasies,' Ampah persuaded Asabea.

Asabea turned down Ampah's proposal, explaining that they went to school to study, but not to engage in a loving relationship. She also explained that a boy-girl relationship in senior high school is bogus; it ends when those involved complete school.

Nonetheless, upon Ampah's continuous proposals to her, she accepted it, but on the condition that they would not indulge in a sexual relationship until they married. Asabea explained that they were young for sex. When they entered into a serious platonic relationship, their love for each other blossomed with the passage of time.

Two weeks before they completed school, their relationship was indefinitely sealed after Bimpong had gone to Ampah to have a conversation with him.

'Ampah, I sense danger. Do you really love Asabea?' Bimpong asked.

'Yes,' Ampah replied.

'Good! Does she also love you?' Bimpong inquired.

'Yes,' Ampah retorted.

'You are lying. Don't deceive yourself. If she loves you, what shows? You should test her whether she truly loves you,' Bimpong suggested.

'Why are you asking me these questions?' Ampah demanded.

'I sense danger for you; I sense that somebody will snatch Asabea from you just after completing school, so you must work against it else you will lose her forever. You must not act as her bodyguard for someone to come and snatch her from you,' said Bimpong.

'How can I work against it?' Ampah asked.

'Blood covenant will do,' Bimpong suggested.

'What? Blood covenant? No. it is evil to do it,' Ampah remarked.

'You must not be timid; you must behave like a man. What is evil about this? Is it a murder? People have done it and they have survived. How can't you do it and also survive peacefully? If Asabea really loves you, she has to do it. If she doesn't do it, it means she has the intention to abandon you like a toilet paper after you complete school,' Bimpong explained.

'I don't think we can do it,' Ampah remarked.

'If you know that you are not going to disappoint each other, why should you fear to undertake an activity which is a guarantee that you are not going to disappoint each other,' Bimpong asserted.

Ampah, who was intoxicated by love and entertained the fears that somebody might snatch Asabea from him, agreed to make a blood covenant with her to keep them inseparable and faithful to each other. Thus, on the next day, Ampah met Asabea behind the library where they stood under an orange tree which was near the bush.

'Do you love me?' Ampah asked in a sonorous voice.

'Yes. Why do you doubt my love for you?' asked Asabea.

'I don't doubt your love for me. I want us to make erm…blood covenant,' Ampah stammered.

'What? Blood covenant? No. What has come over you?' Asabea said in astonishment.

'There is nothing to fear. Blood covenant has no bad effects. It is just a mere exchange of blood. Symbolically, it is a promise that we will not disappoint each other and I want to prove to you beyond all reasonable doubts that I'll remain faithful to you until death separates us. People have done it and they experienced no harm, so why should you fear? What is harmful about sealing our relationship with our own blood?' Ampah said.

Asabea who was also intoxicated by love and wanted to prove to Ampah that she truly loved him agreed to make the blood covenant. Thus, they met in the bush behind the library and made the blood covenant to consolidate and seal their relationship. They used a blade to cut small parts of their thumbs to ooze blood and crossed the thumbs for their blood to mix.

'Today, we hereby say with one accord that we are true lovers and that we will marry and be faithful to each other until death separates us,' they sworn and licked the blood on their thumbs.

'So be it,' they concluded.

As time went by, Ampah and Asabea completed senior high school and passed their examinations with flying colours. They, therefore, went to the same university so that they would not be geographically separated from each other. At the university, their love for each other reached its climax so they did most activities together. During their leisure time, they would play games such as Ludo, see-saw, snooker, and hide and seek. They also visited interesting places and shared moments of joy together.

After graduating from university, Asabea was employed as an accountant in a reputable bank at Accra while Ampah pursued a master's degree in Law after which he worked as a law lecturer at university. At the age of twenty-nine, Ampah achieved excellence in the academic world and reached the top of the academic ladder; he obtained a doctorate degree in Law.

Ampah and Asabea then decided to marry in order to legalize their long-established relationship. Preparations were made to contract the marriage. Since Ampah did not know his biological mother and family backgrounds and his biological father, Amoako was in the United States of America, Obeng and his wife, Fosuah, who took care of him, represented him as his parents for the marriage ceremony. Ampah explained that Obeng and his wife were his parents because they took care of him from basic school to doctorate degree level, so it would not be out of place if they arranged, organized and contracted marriage for him without the presence of his unknown biological mother and relatives.

To oil the wheels of tradition, Obeng and his wife together with other people went to ask for Asabea's hand in marriage from her relatives in Pimso and a time was fixed for the wedding ceremony. Accordingly, Obeng informed Ampah's father who was in the United States of America about the wedding ceremony and when it would be held.

When the wedding ceremony was held, a huge crowd of people including eminent people such as university professors, magistrates, lawyers, doctors, bank managers, university lecturers and accountants attended it. There were massive jubilations, enjoyment, socialization, exchange of gifts and donations in cedis, pounds, dollars and euros.

However, the overwhelming joy that had engulfed the wedding ceremony was short-lived when Ampah's biological father, Amoako, came from the United states of America and appeared at the scene at the time Ampah and Asabea were about to take the marriage vow.

'What abomination is this? This is a big mistake,' Amoako shouted in desperation when he saw the mother and the relatives of Ampah's prospective wife. Unknown to everybody at the scene, Ampah and Asabea were the twins of Amoako and his divorced wife, Ansaba who had met in a senior high school to enter into a relationship leading to marriage. Since Ampah and Asabea had been identified as twins, they could not be allowed to marry according to the customs and traditions of the people.

'It's an abomination for twins to marry each other. We can't allow it to happen. We will not only invite troubles to the twins, but also bring curses to our community if we allow Ampah and Asabea to marry,' an old man remarked.

When Ampah and Asabea got to know that there were twins, they fell unconscious, but they were rushed to hospital for treatment before they gained consciousness.

'What a mistaken love? What a big mistake? What a mistaken love? What problem is this?' Ampah lamented when he gained consciousness.

Ampah and Asabea pleaded that they should be allowed to marry whether or not they were twins since they loved each other, but many people vehemently condemned and opposed their decision.

'It is against our traditions and customs as well as modern civilization for twins to marry each other. To allow twins to marry each other in the name of mistaken love has a lot of negative effects which we cannot bear. It is a taboo to allow twins to marry each other,' the people said.

Ampah and Asabea were helpless and they could neither eat well nor have sound sleep, so they grew lean each day.

CHAPTER FIFTEEN

Three weeks later, Ampah and Asabea fell sick; some strange rashes appeared on their skins and they became deaf and dumb.

'Eh! What has come over Ampah and Asabea? Is the effect of not allowing them to marry?' their mother, Ansaba remarked as she shed tears.

'Don't cry. Your children will be well. It is too much worries and thinking that have made them sick,' Ansaba's brother, Kobina consoled her.

Ampah and Asabea were rushed to hospital for treatment, but they did not get well; their conditions became worse.

'If Ampah and Asabea can't be cured with unorthodox medicines, we should try orthodox medicines. Deafness and dumbness are diseases which are not meant to be cured with unorthodox medicines; they are normally cured with orthodox medicines,' their maternal grandmother, Konadu, suggested.

Ampah and Asabea were, then, taken to an herbalist, Safo in a village, Bansi. Safo was very old and had knowledge of herbs. It was said that he could combine some herbs to ignite fire and could use herbs to heal the dumb, the paralytic and the deaf. He was also a soothsayer who could tell by divination some events which would happen in the future. After he had poured water into a bottle and corked it, he lifted it up and gazed into it for some few minutes. When he recited incantations, the water in the bottle boiled and changed to red.

'O-o-o-o-oh! Sssssh! It is clear before my eyes. Ampah and Asabea have brought curses to themselves. Their predicaments are the result of what they did many years ago. A-a-a-ah! The truth is before my eyes; Ampah and Asabea had made a blood covenant to marry and be faithful to each other until death. Their refusal to fulfill the blood covenant is cause of their predicaments,' Safo revealed.

'What can be done to save their lives,' Amoako inquired.

'Nothing can be done. They will die in four days,' Safo retorted.

News and information about the impending death of Ampah and Asabea were the topic of discussion in many places. All hope was lost and the people had no option than to anticipate the death of Ampah and Asabea since it had been foretold by Safo, a well-known soothsayer.

When the four days elapsed, a great tragedy struck the people of Pimso. There were wailings, weeping, lamentations, ululations and expressing of condolences here and there. Tears streamed down the faces of people. Ampah and Asabea did not wake up when they slept and they could not be awoken; they lay motionless on their beds.

'I'm in trouble. I'm doomed. My children, Ampah, a university lecturer and Asabea, an accountant are dead. What a tragedy?' Ansaba lamented while she rolled on the ground and wailed to invite people to the house.

Within an hour, a huge crowd of people had gathered in the house to peep at Ampah and Asabea, the twins who were mistakenly in love.

'Eh! This is strange. It has never happened in Pimso for twins to die at the same time. This is strange. This is beyond human understanding,' a grey-bearded man,' Amponsa lamented.

'How can twins died at the same time? The death of Ampah and Asabea is not ordinary; it may have a spiritual cause,' another man remarked.

At 4:00pm, the family members met at the house where the bodies of Ampah and Asabea had been kept to plan for their burial. During the meeting, pandemonium broke out and there was a stampede; people rushed out of the house to seek refuge. Some of them were falling to the ground while others were also falling over bottles, chairs and tables.

'Ghost! Ghost o-o-o-o ghost!' the people shouted as they ran to seek refuge. Ampah and Asabea appeared at the meeting while the meeting was going on. They looked helpless and wondered what was going on when they saw people in mourning clothes and why people shouted, 'Ghost o-o-o-o ghost!'

Unknown to everybody, Ampah and Asabea did not die; they fell into coma and the people mistook them to be dead since they were expecting their deaths as foretold by a well-known soothsayer. While people ran away from the meeting place when they saw Ampah and Asabea, a group of prayer warriors led by a prophet of God called Daning from a nearby town went to the place. The group led by Prophet Daning summoned the parents and the relatives of Ampah and Asabea.

'During prayers requested for Ampah and Asabea by a member of my prayer group for their unfortunate conditions, it was revealed to me by God that spells had been cast on them by forces of darkness to be deaf and dumb and fall into coma and die eventually. The spirit of God has, therefore, commissioned us to come and pray for them because, today, salvation is theirs,' Prophet Daning explained.

'Amen!' the people shouted in unison.

Without delay, Ampah and Asabea were brought before the prayer warriors led by Prophet Daning who could heal the blind, the lame, the deaf and exorcize evil spirits from people in the name of Jesus.

'Acts 4:12; *salvation is found in no-one else, for there is no other name under heaven given to men by which we must be saved,*' Prophet Daning quoted and moved forth and back while he was holding his Bible. He asked his prayer warriors to pray for forgiveness of sins on behalf of Ampah and Asabea and ask God to heal them. While some of them clapped as they prayed, others also spoke in tongues. Ampah and Asabea, who could not stand on their feet when they were buffeted and caught up by spirit of God, fell to the ground and rolled from one place to the other repeatedly.

'I deliver you from all forms of physical and spiritual attacks and break any blood covenant you have made and its effects on you in the name of Jesus. I heal you of deafness and dumbness in the name of Jesus,' Prophet Daning prayed.

In fact, prayer in the name of Jesus is a terrific terror that terrifies terrible terrors. When Prophet Daning prayed for

Ampah and Asabea, something mysterious happened; some starchy-like fluids flowed from their noses and they began to talk while at the same time vapour oozed from their ears and they began to hear.

'Praise the Lord for healing Ampah and Asabea!' Prophet Daning shouted.

'Amen!' the prayer warriors and the people responded.

'The fluids from their noses and the vapour from their ears are the manifestation of the spells which were cast on them by forces of darkness,' Prophet Daning explained.

Prophet Daning together with his prayer warriors as well as the people who were at the place sang songs of praises to glorify God for healing Ampah and Asabea and for saving them from an impending death. That day, many people including Ampah and Asabea as well as their divorced parents, Amoako and Ansaba, became Christians. Consequently, they lived an exemplary Christian life worthy of emulation.

Mistaken Love